I0564021

LOVE SONGS

THE KELLER FAMILY SERIES ~ BOOK FIVE

BERNADETTE MARIE

5 PRINCE PUBLISHING

4th Edition 2021

Published by 5 Prince Publishing, PO Box 865, Arvada, CO 80001

www.5PrinceBooks.com

Digital ISBN: 978-1-939217-77-6

Print ISBN: 9978-1-939217-78-3

❀ Created with Vellum

To Stan,
My books are my love songs for you!

ACKNOWLEDGMENTS

To my 5,
    You inspire me to be better every day!

To Mom, Dad, and Sissy,
    I love you. This family I write about is great because
    I have you all to draw from.

To Randy Sayner,
    How can I say thank you enough for sharing your talent with
me, your songs, and your wisdom! You made this book what it is
and we're blessed to have you in our lives!

To June,
    How many times have you come to my rescue? Chalk up
another one. I can't believe how lucky we were to get you in our
lives in 2003! I've had you by my side longer than Mr. J! You are a
blessing!

To Country Music
    Country music makes me happy and so do those who sing it.
Thank you to Tim McGraw, Luke Bryan, Blake Shelton, Carrie
Underwood, Dierks Bently and all the other performers I
mention in my books. Your music inspires me. And to Dan and
Shay, your story made me realize there was a fabulous ending to
this book!

ALSO BY BERNADETTE MARIE

THE MATCHMAKER SERIES

Matchmakers

Encore

Finding Hope

THE THREE MRS. MONROES TRILOGY

Amelia

Penelope

Vivian

THE ASPEN CREEK SERIES

First Kiss

Unexpected Admirer

On Thin Ice

Indomitable Spirit

THE DENVER BRIDE SERIES

Cart Before the Horse

Never Saw it Coming

Candy Kisses

ROMANTIC SUSPENSE

Chasing Shadows

PARANORMAL ROMANCES

The Tea Shop

The Last Goodbye

HOLIDAY FAVORITES

Corporate Christmas

Tropical Christmas

Date for Hire

THE DEVEREAUX FAMILY SERIES

Kennedy Devereaux

Chase Devereaux

Max Devereaux

Paige Devereaux

FUNERALS AND WEDDINGS SERIES

Something Lost

Something Discovered

Something Found

Something Forbidden

Something New

LOVE SONGS

CHAPTER 1

*C*ould the sun possibly be any hotter, or brighter, or…

Warner's brakes screeched as he came to a stop at the stoplight he'd nearly run though. The glare from the hood of his Ford was blinding. The sweat on his neck was annoying. And the fact that he'd just been told he had no talent, well that was pissing him off.

He had talent. He had a butt-load of talent. Warner Wright had performed on every stage in Nashville. Oh, he'd performed with some of the biggest names when they were begging for a job.

He let out a breath. So why had he been passed up?

Oh he knew why!

The reputation of his family came long before he started trying to sell his songs. One thing about being the ex-stepson of Patricia Little, was all of Nashville knew she was trouble. And even if you were a thirty year old man, and you hadn't had the woman in your life since your own father committed suicide when you were twelve, those things stick in the minds of some. It didn't help that after his father's death, she married a little bigger —a little richer—and soon she'd made it into the bed of The OX,

Harley Oxbury. The only problem was he was Nashville royalty —and married to Nashville royalty. The legend was when Christine Eaden found out about Harley and Patricia she put a shotgun to his crotch and threatened to dismember him.

Did it matter to the world that his ex-stepmother took down one of Nashville's icons? Oh, yeah. The OX lost his career. Record companies didn't want him anymore. The public didn't want to see his shows. There wasn't a product willing to put his name out front. Patricia Little had ruined the icon and her reputation, twenty years later, she was tarnishing his.

Perhaps he needed to change his name.

That was stupid. His name was fine. The woman was only his step mother for two years. By now the town should have forgotten the men she left in her path. Well they probably would have if she hadn't gone on TV and done one of those reality shows where Warner's picture was prominently displayed on her mantel as some kind of trophy of the husbands and "others'" children she left in her wake. And hadn't he asked the producers to take that down? Only a million times.

Well, some people were meant to be on stage and some behind the scenes. The guitar on the passenger seat was a reminder that he was one of them.

Although Jordan Farr, the head of Master Records, told him if he could get a voice to back up his music, maybe the world would start to see past his relation to Patricia Little. That had been the most positive feedback he'd received yet.

The light turned green and Warner eased off the clutch and onto the gas. The truck hiccupped and then picked up speed.

But in Nashville afternoon traffic, he didn't make it far. Warner eased to a stop at the next light.

He could hear the music which the city had been built on. It poured out of the stores and the bars. But this music was closer and the voice wasn't Carrie Underwood's or Miranda Lambert's. No this was fresh, sweet, original, and very close.

Warner turned his head to the right and spotted a woman in a Jeep tapping her fingers on the steering wheel. The song wasn't one he'd heard on the radio. It wasn't a karaoke cut either. No, she was singing to someone's music, and she was magnificent.

She turned her head as if she might have felt his stare. Her dark hair was pulled back in a ponytail. The aviator glasses shielding her eyes reflected his beat-up blue pickup truck.

She stopped singing and smiled. And it wasn't just any smile. It was the kind that came with a wink, if he could have seen her eyes.

That moment nearly stopped his heart, just as her voice had. If he had her by his side then the doors of this town would open up to him.

The woman eased through the intersection and turned right at the next light.

He had to follow.

Warner checked his mirrors and quickly changed lanes. It was a close call with a Mustang, of all things, and the driver flipped him the middle finger. But he had to keep her in his sight.

He made a right, but her Jeep wasn't on the street.

"Damn!" He smacked the steering wheel.

But just then he saw the Jeep. The woman was climbing out of it.

Warner made a U-turn, again causing a car to blare its horn at him and that driver to flip him off. The heat must be getting to everyone. They were all in such a nasty mood.

She'd parked in front of a theater and was jogging up the steps.

Warner screeched to a halt in the middle of the street and pulled his brake. The woman turned around on the steps of the theater and stopped.

He climbed across the bench seat to the passenger door and hung his head out the window.

"Hey," he yelled like some back woods yokel.

"Hey, yourself." She had an accent. She was native and that might be iffy. If she grew up in Nashville then she knew all about the shame of his family. But he'd let that find its own moment. This one was his.

"I'm not stalking you. I swear."

"If you say so," she said slowly, but she didn't make a move toward the street and he didn't blame her.

"I heard you singing. You're freaking amazing."

She laughed and her ponytail waved behind her. "I appreciate that."

"No, really. I know what I'm talking about." He tried to open the door, but it wasn't going so well.

She'd taken another step toward the building. He was losing her.

"Wait. I want to talk to you." Finally he managed the handle and nearly fell out of the truck, which he'd left running

The woman had made it to the top of the steps and gripped the knob on the front door of the theater.

"I'm not crazy. Please hear me out," he was begging, but at least common sense had kicked in enough and he stopped moving toward her. "I'm a song writer. I'm looking for a voice."

The woman nodded slowly, but she didn't make any more moves to run away. That was a positive sign, wasn't it?

"What's your name?" she called down to him.

"Warner. Warner Wright."

"Warner Wright the song writer? Cute."

"No, that's really my name." He took one step further toward the curb. "You have an amazing voice."

She looked at the watch on her wrist then back up at him. "You gathered that from hearing me in my truck?"

"Yes."

Again, she nodded slowly. "Listen, I'm going to be late. If you want to come in and sit that's fine. But I'm out of time for talking on the street."

She opened the door to the theater and walked inside.

Warner started for the door and then the grumbling of his truck caught his attention. God, was he this desperate?

He hurried back to the truck, climbed in, and parked it down the street.

CHAPTER 2

*C*lara locked her purse up in her aunt's office and headed for rehearsal. The man in the street had scared the hell out of her at first, but she'd lived in Nashville her whole life. Every song writer thought they had what it took to make it big. Some of them got desperate enough to hunt down talent. But she'd never heard of this approach.

He hadn't come inside. Perhaps he'd given up. All the same, she had her cell phone in her pocket. The theater had once been gutted by fire because of a psycho man. She didn't care to see that repeated.

On the stage was a small ensemble waiting for her arrival. Behind them, the set to West Side Story was being repositioned for the weekend's production.

"Thought you gave up on us," Duke shouted from the piano. "You only have four shows left. Don't give up now," he laughed.

"The only reason I wouldn't show up is because it's too damn hot in here," she said as she made it to the side of the stage. She walked up the stairs and joined the others.

Duke gave her a nod. "Let's just take it from the top and work the songs. Arianna wants these last four shows to be sharp."

They had only started the first song when the door opened and Warner walked into the theater. Why she thought he might be a threat she didn't know because looking at him now she thought he looked like the biggest nerd she'd ever seen.

His jeans were worn, his shirt was untucked, and his thick blond hair was messed up something awful. More than likely he'd been driving all day with his windows down.

He'd helped himself to a seat in the back and just listened as they practiced. Well, she thought, if he liked what he heard in the car wait till he heard her sing as Maria.

WARNER WONDERED HOW LONG HE'D SAT IN THAT THEATER, ALONE. He was familiar with the musical—very familiar. They'd just finished the number *Somewhere*. Damn, he'd listened to nearly the entire musical. But that voice. She had the goods!

"She's something, huh?"

Warner jumped in his seat and looked at the man next to him. Quickly he got to his feet. "Um, yes. She's amazing."

"That's my niece."

"She has a fantastic voice." Warner turned to the man and held out his hand. He didn't want this man to think he was crazy. "I'm Warner Wright. I'm a song writer. I heard her sing in the street and wanted to talk to her."

The man nodded. "John Forrester." He turned and looked at the woman he'd followed into the theater. "She doesn't know you?"

"No, sir. But I'm not stalking her. I just wanted to talk to her about singing."

John nodded slowly again and pulled his hand back. "She's trained with a gun."

Warner swallowed hard. "Most women in Tennessee are, sir."

That made John laugh. "True enough." He patted Warner on the shoulder. "She's almost through."

He gave him a smile and then looked toward the stage and gave his niece a glance. A million words were said between them in that moment, he wondered what they were.

Warner sat back down in his seat and listened as they finished the rest of the show.

To say he was moved would be an understatement. A piano and a dozen voices could do amazing things.

When the group stood up they all began to talk. This was a family, a musical family. One brought together by a common love and the current show they produced together.

It had been years since Warner was in musical theater, but you never forgot the feeling.

The woman he'd followed walked away from the group and was headed toward him. Her thumbs were tucked into the front pockets of her cutoff jeans.

The eyes which had hid behind the shiny aviators, which were now hung from the front of her tank top, were dark brown.

Warner quickly stood.

"You followed me all the way in here and listened to rehearsal?" Her accent was drawn out.

"Yes. I have to say, you're amazing."

The woman nodded slowly, just as her uncle had done. "You've said that, but thank you." She looked down at her bare toes in the sandals she wore and wiggled them. The middle ones had rings on them. "Is that all you wanted to tell me?"

"Yes. No. I—is there somewhere we can talk?"

She looked around. "What's wrong with here?"

"Right. Listen, I'm a song writer and I'm looking for a voice to demo my work."

"And you're looking for lessons?"

Warner raked his fingers through his hair. It was getting much too long. He looked down at his attire. God, she must think I'm a hobo.

"No. I'm not looking for lessons. I'm looking for someone to do the vocals."

"And you want me to do that?"

He smiled. Finally they were on the same page. "Yes."

"I see. Mr. Wright, I'm very busy with the theater right now. I just don't…"

"Would you just look at them?" He was so desperate he was hunting down strangers to sing his songs. This was embarrassing. "Please. Maybe just a few hours with me and you could see what you think."

"You don't even know my name."

He dropped his shoulders. He was desperate.

He held out his hand to shake hers. "Again, I'm Warner Wright."

She smiled and took his hand. Her grip was firm. There was no messing around with this one. "Clara Keller."

"Ms. Keller, I would appreciate a moment of your time to show you my work."

She pulled her hand back, tucked it into her back pocket and gave him a regarding look.

"Do you know where the Riverside Building is?"

He raised his eyebrow. "Doesn't everyone? This is Nashville."

She chuckled. "There is a Starbucks on the main floor. I'll meet you there tomorrow at ten."

"Tomorrow at ten. Starbucks. Riverside Building."

"Will that work?"

He nodded. "Thank you. Can I take you out for a drink tonight? No business, just get to know you?"

Clara pulled her phone out of her back pocket. "Thanks, but I have one guilty pleasure and it's on TV tonight."

A bead of sweat rolled down the back of his neck. He forced a smile. "What might that be?"

"Reality TV at its worse. Ever heard of Nashville Ex-wives Club?"

He knew the blood had just drained out of his head. Damn if he fainted this would be over.

"I've heard of it."

"Never miss a one. That Little woman is such trash she makes me laugh. But I'll see you tomorrow. Ten."

He only nodded as Clara left the theater.

Well, this was over. Once Clara found out about his connection with Patricia Little, she too would exit stage left.

Warner left the theater just in time to see a tow truck drive away with his pickup.

It was official—Nashville hated him.

CHAPTER 3

arner had been in the Riverside Building numerous times. When one was a courier, every building in downtown was familiar. Those days seemed much easier now as he walked through revolving doors.

He knew it was hot, but he was sweating more than normal. It was stupid. He'd sat in front of music execs that could make or break him. So why did this woman, whom he didn't know, make him so nervous?

A glance at his watch and he realized it was ten o'clock straight up. He'd hoped to have been there a few minutes early, but then again, that wouldn't be his style. He was just lucky he wasn't late.

Clara was already there seated by the front bank of windows. There was an iced coffee drink in front of her and she was looking at her iPhone.

When he approached the table she looked up at him and gave him a grin. It wasn't a smile—it was a grin and that did something funny to his stomach.

"Mornin'," she drawled out.

"Mornin'."

"I got here early with my brother, so I already have had two coffees. Hope you don't mind I started without you."

He shook his head. "No, that's fine. I don't drink coffee. Your brother works in the building?"

She sat back in her seat and the grin turned into a smile. He was humoring her with his sporadic talking in circles.

"He works in a corner office upstairs."

"Corner office?" He sat his bag on an empty chair. "He must be important."

Clara shrugged. "I suppose. So what did you want to show me?"

That was more like it. Get down to business and stop trying to make small talk. So far she hadn't said anything about his picture prominently displayed on the mantel of Patricia Little's home during last night's episode of that trashy show, so maybe she hadn't noticed, or maybe she'd missed it. Could he be so lucky? After all, he'd caught it and it hadn't helped that Patricia mentioned him by name and called him untalented.

Warner pulled out the chair and sat down. It wasn't but a split second later he realized he still had his sling bag over him and it was choking him. He tried to finesse his way from under the strap and pull it over his head, but the strap caught his sunglasses, which were now stuck in his hair.

There was the great possibility that he was going to hang himself before he got to show her any of his work. This was so stupid.

He managed the bag over his head and he was sure he heard his glasses crack. The bag fell to the floor with a grand thud. There were probably a few cracked CDs in there now. Great!

Warner reached for his sunglasses and tried to pull them from his hair without leaving a huge hole from the number of strands he could feel himself pull out.

Finally, he was free of his captor and the torture device—his sunglasses—which looked only slightly bent out of shape.

Now he had to make eye contact with this beautiful woman across from him and hope she wasn't laughing.

Her gaze was out the window. She hadn't seen him at all.

Thank God!

She turned her head back toward him. "So, show me your work."

"Right." He tucked the bent glasses into the front of his shirt and reached for his bag. He unzipped it carefully, hoping the contents wouldn't spill out all over the floor, as that seemed to be how things in his life were going.

The sheets of music he'd brought with him had taken the form of the folder, which had curled up in the bag. Well, it was just paper.

He slid them across the table to her.

Clara picked them up as she tucked her leg under her. She liked things casual, this came across loud and clear. There was no diva mentality built into her. She was very comfortable in her skin and he wished he was equally as comfortable in his.

She tapped her fingers on the table as she looked over the music. It was playing in her head, he knew what that looked like. No one had to tell him she was musically inclined. It radiated from her like the confidence she exuded.

Her lips twitched as she read, as if she were singing the song. The mangled CDs might be worthless—she didn't need them.

Clara flipped to the next page and went through the same motions, but then she tilted her head as if something didn't make sense. But she kept going, her head bobbing to the beat she obviously heard in her head.

Warner had his hands clasped tightly under the table as he watched her. It had been almost five minutes and she hadn't said a word.

Again she flipped to the next song and this time she smiled.

"Someone jade you? This one screams revenge."

He gritted his teeth. "Ex-stepmother. She's wicked."

The smile on her lips grew and then she bit down on her lip and nodded. "These are amazing," she said as she lay down the papers.

"You really think so?"

"Yeah. The melodies are great. The music is fluid. I like them."

"Will you record them—for demo?"

Clara tilted her head and gave him a long look of consideration. Then she picked up her drink and took a small sip before setting it back down. "You really haven't heard me perform."

"I listened to your entire rehearsal."

"That is totally different." She picked up the music again and sorted through it. She pulled out one piece and looked it over before laying it atop the rest. "I like this one the best."

"Love Song? Why?"

She laughed. "Because it isn't your normal love song. The guy is a bumbling idiot, but all because he's in love with a girl. I like that."

He felt the blood drain from his face. She just might be the most perfect woman in the world. The girl he'd written the song about didn't care for his bumbling idiot ways.

"Do you have plans tomorrow night?" she asked.

Warner shook his head.

"I'm playing at The Stage with a friend. Come see me really sing."

He hadn't actually thought she was a performer, not like that. He'd been so mesmerized by her voice in the truck he'd forgotten that she might actually be someone who was just like everyone else and wanted fame and fortune in Nashville. Why would she want to help him?

He nodded his acceptance to the invitation.

A man came up to the window behind her and tapped on it. She turned, smiled, and gave him a wave.

He gave Warner a nod and though he tried to smile, Warner

was sure he smirked at the man. There was a case at the man's feet. It looked like a banjo.

Wow, he could pick them. Beautiful woman with an amazing voice, who was already a performer with some boyfriend who wore his hair long and a bandanna like a rock star. Warner might as well go find a bicycle and become a courier again. With any luck he could be hit by a delivery truck the first week.

Clara held up a finger to the man and he nodded. "I have to go."

"Sure. Sure."

She looked down at the song. "You'll come and listen to us tomorrow?"

"Us?"

"Me and Randy. Randy Seymour—heard of him?"

That was a name going around Nashville like a wild fire. "Sure, I've heard of him."

She nodded to the man who had turned to watch the people in the plaza. "He's got the goods."

Warner felt his stomach tighten.

Clara swung her bag over her shoulder. "Can I borrow this?" She picked up the piece of music and looked it over again. "I'll give it back, I promise."

Oh, hell. What did he have to lose? This beautiful woman was going to steal his song and he was going to get run over by a delivery truck. No fretting there.

"Sure."

"Thanks." She picked up her drink and took another sip. "I like you. You're cute."

Certainly that hadn't been what he thought she'd say. "Thank you," the words choked out.

"I'll see you tomorrow. We start at seven-thirty."

"Okay."

She turned to walk away and then turned back. "Hey, Warner,

just for the record. I don't think you're a talentless moron. I think that title belongs to Patricia Little."

With a wink Clara was gone and Warner was sure he was going to lose consciousness and fall right out of his chair.

Clara knew exactly who he was. Crap!

CHAPTER 4

*C*lara walked through the door and out to the plaza where Randy stood watching people walk by. She looked back into the Starbucks where Warner shoved papers back into his bag.

"What's with the guy?" Randy asked as they started down the street.

"Song writer. Wants me to demo his work for him."

Randy nodded. "Nice."

"He's cute too."

Randy looked back. "Just your style. Blond and a complete mess."

"What does that mean?"

He laughed. "You would die if you married a suit."

Clara nodded. "You're right." She handed him the song she'd borrowed from Warner. "This is one of his pieces."

Randy took the paper and looked it over. Obviously the song played in his head as he read it. "This is good."

"It is, isn't it?" She took it back and looked it over. "Think we can pull this together and perform it tomorrow?"

"It's simple enough."

She thought of the look Warner would have on his face when he heard his song. That would be priceless.

Then she thought about putting him to the true test of who he was. The entire Keller family would be there to see her and Randy perform. Warner could certainly use a dose of family, she was sure. It had to be horrible to have lost your father, and your step-mother was some reality TV show hag.

In the right hands, Warner Wright could be a super star. In her hands, he could be taken care of.

There was a tightening in her chest as Randy grabbed her hand and pulled her across the street. Why did she want to take care of Warner Wright?

CLARA HADN'T NOTICED SHE WAS HUNGRY UNTIL RANDY mentioned stopping into a small diner before they rehearsed. She hadn't eaten breakfast. She'd only downed those coffee drinks and now she was shaky. It wasn't quite lunch time, but that didn't seem to faze Randy. Then again, not much did.

She'd ordered eggs and toast, but she didn't realize she really hadn't eaten much when Randy reached across the table, grabbed hold of her hand, and stopped her from just pushing her eggs around.

"What's up with you today?" he asked releasing her hand.

She set down her fork. "Do you know who Warner Wright is?"

"That guy you met at Starbucks?"

"Yeah. Did you recognize him?"

Randy bit into his toast. "Should I?"

"You know who Patricia Little is, right?"

"Hag."

She snorted a laugh. Who in Nashville didn't know Patricia Little? She'd wrecked the OX's career. No one was going to forget that.

"Have you ever seen her show?"

"That reality show? Are you kidding me? Why rot my brain?"

Even though she agreed with him, she just couldn't help herself. "Well, see, when they interview Patricia Little she's always in front of her fireplace. And on her mantel she has all of these family pictures." She began stirring her eggs again. "I'm not sure what the point of the family pictures are. I mean, none of the kids are hers. She doesn't talk nice about any of them anyway."

"Clara, you're not making much sense."

No, she wasn't. "Warner Wright is one of Patricia Little's step-children."

Randy stopped chewing and just stared at her. Then he swallowed hard. "The man who wants you to sing his songs is the step-son of the woman who took down the OX and ruined his career?"

"In all fairness, he's her ex-step-son."

"Not sure that's comforting."

Clara set down her fork again. "I don't think he has anything to do with her. I mean wouldn't he have mentioned it?"

Randy shrugged.

Clara thought about the song and about the man. Her family had secrets too—scandal even. But nothing compared to that of Patricia Little's drama.

She pulled her phone out of her pocket and began searching for information.

"What are you doing?" Randy choked out.

"Looking for information. Why is his picture still in her house? How long ago was she married to his dad?"

"Why does this matter?"

"I don't know. I like him."

"Why?"

Clara looked up at him and smiled. "He's just my type right?"

Randy laughed. "You're a mess."

Clara searched for Patricia Little's husband with the last name of Wright. Lewis Wright had been her second husband. "Oh, God."

"What? Did he ruin someone's career too?"

She looked up at him. Tears were welling in her eyes. "His father committed suicide."

"Damn."

"That's the saddest thing I've ever heard."

"You know what I hear in all this? He has baggage."

"I have baggage."

Randy wiped his mouth with his napkin and then threw it at her. "Clara Keller has no baggage."

She bit down on her lip. He was right. She might come from the most eclectic family ever assembled, but her life had been squeaky clean. The only drama that had ever come about in her life was her mother's cancer, which she beat, and most recently the admission that her brother's fiancée was actually the baby her aunt had given up for adoption. Okay, when she thought about it, that did sound like some television drama. Though it just wasn't that way. Her family wasn't that way. The only person who was having a hard time dealing with her brother Ed's fiancée was her cousin Tyler. But even he understood it, even if he did find it hard to deal with.

"Do you think I'm crazy to want to help him?"

"Yes."

She dropped her shoulders. "That was a very definite answer."

"You like to perform. You like to be on stage at the theater. He's asking you to record."

"So."

"So, that's not what you've wanted all this time."

He was right. It sucked to have a best friend who knew you so well.

"It's not like he wants me to be the talent for his songs. He just wants me to be the voice on the demo."

Randy shook his head. "You're going to fall for this guy and you're going to get hurt."

"I am not."

"Not what? Going to fall or get hurt?"

She didn't like how this conversation was going and worse she didn't like that she couldn't answer him.

Perhaps she needed to get to know him better. After all, she knew nothing except for what Patricia Little told the whole world on her trashy reality show.

Tomorrow, after the show, she'd get to know Warner Wright, but for now she needed to convince Randy to buy her breakfast. She had just realized she'd used all her money on Starbucks.

CHAPTER 5

*O*nly in Nashville could a bar be packed on a Wednesday night when the entertainment wasn't a big name.

Warner figured he could very easily get lost in the crowd which had gathered at The Stage, but the only table open was only feet from the stage under the enormous mural that decorated the wall.

He made his way through the people and sat down.

"Oh, no. I already have a seat for you," the charming voice he'd already fallen in love with spoke from behind him.

Warner turned to find Clara Keller, in a flowy white shirt and hip hugging jeans, standing behind him in some angelic glow with the lights illuminating the red highlights in her hair.

He felt the hair on the back of his neck stand up. That was a lot to observe when all he wanted to do was hear the woman sing.

"You have a seat for me?"

Clara pointed to the raised seating area just behind him where all the tables had been pushed together and every seat was taken, but one. "Your seat awaits among my fans."

Warner's palms began to sweat. He recognized the man from

the theater, her uncle. Oh, dear Lord! If that was her uncle, and they were all staring at him with grins on their faces, this must be her family. Was the woman crazy? She wanted him to sit with her family? He wasn't ready for that. He wasn't ready for any of this. God, no wonder they kept kicking him out of record exec's offices. If he was a mess like this now, how could he possibly think he could have an artist criticize his work and change it?

He swallowed hard. He should be used to being under a microscope. Patricia Little had put him under one.

Seriously, he was having second thoughts about all this. Again, the bike courier job seemed like a better deal—in New York!

Clara took his hand and led him toward the group. The first man to stand narrowed his eyes at him. Warner's mouth went dry.

"Warner, this is my father Carlos."

The man extended his hand toward him and Warner shook it. "It's nice to meet you, sir."

"Likewise. So my little girl is going to help you with your songs?"

Oh, he felt little. "Yes. I think she is."

Clara smiled at him. "He's got some talent, Dad."

"Well, wait until you really hear her." Carlos smiled down at Clara and wrapped a protective arm around her shoulders.

Clara pointed to a chair on the other side of the table. "You can sit there. That's my brother Christian." The man lifted his hand in a wave. "And my other brother Ed and his fiancée Darcy." She looked at them all. "Is everyone here?"

Darcy pursed her lips and looked around. "All but Tyler."

"I thought he was coming."

Darcy let out a long breath and Ed took her hand and gave it a squeeze. "He doesn't seem to feel very much like doing family things."

There was a hesitation in her voice and Warner picked up on

that right away. He'd heard that resonate from every person he'd ever been related to.

Clara turned to him. "Christian can introduce you to everyone."

There was a whistle from the stage and both Clara and Warner turned their heads. She again held up a finger to the man who had waited for her outside the Starbucks.

"Sorry to abandon you. But they don't bite."

She gave him a friendly pat on the shoulder and headed toward the man on the stage.

All eyes were on him again and there certainly was the thought that leaving without another word would be the right thing to do. Instead, he sucked up his courage and walked around the table to the empty seat.

Christian and Ed each moved their seats as to give him some room, or to distance themselves. It was Darcy who shifted in front of Ed to speak to him.

"This crowd looks dangerous, but they're really nice."

Warner knew his fear was wearing on his face.

Ed let out a snort. "C'mon. We're supposed to look mean when Clara brings a man to the table."

"Well I'm not her man. I mean we're not seeing each other. Purely a working relationship," Warner clarified.

Christian nodded with a laugh. "Sure. I wonder how long that'll last."

"I beg your pardon?" Warner wasn't sure what a tight family dynamic was supposed to be like, but was this really it?

"You're just her type."

Ed gave a nod in agreement. "I suppose we should just put a stocking up with your name come Christmas."

"What?"

Her brothers laughed and Darcy slapped Ed on the leg. "You seem like a very nice man. And Clara has a type. It just happens that you fit that type."

"Oh." What was that really supposed to mean? "I thought she was with him." He pointed to the man who had met her outside the Starbucks yesterday morning and now who sat with her on the stage, their heads together tuning up their guitars.

"Randy?" Ed chuckled. "Um, no."

"No?"

"They've played together for years. She's the background to his stardom. Just the way she likes it."

That comment made no sense at all, until the music began and her family turned their attention toward Clara.

Randy was the lead guitar. Randy was the voice. This was his show. Clara's voice and guitar added the harmony which made each song complete. They were right. She wasn't the star of the show, but she made the star shine.

The waitress came by and took his drink order, how boring was he to order just a Pepsi, but he wanted to keep his wits about him. Though, halfway through their set he nearly spit the drink out when he heard the familiar melody he'd created.

This time it was Clara's guitar in lead and her voice which resonated through the bar. The tempo had slowed down, the crowd had grown softer, and the eyes of her family had misted to his words. He wrote that song! This was the song she had borrowed and dear Lord, she made it sound good.

How was it that fate worked in such ways? She was just a person in a passing car. And now he could frankly fall in love with her. He wasn't going to—but he could.

Randy hadn't added much but an underlying hum where appropriate and a shift in the harmony, which worked. It wasn't how Warner would have done it, but damn it was genius!

When the song was over the bar erupted into an applause which burst through him. They'd loved it. They really loved it.

"Thank ya'll for that. I borrowed that song from a very talented song writer yesterday. I think he'll do well with it." Her accent had deepened when she spoke to the audience. Then she looked his way. "Everyone give it up for Warner Wright."

The crowd applauded, but he was all too familiar with the quick whispers which accompanied his name.

Look, it's the step-son of Patricia Little—the woman who ruined the OX.

The set continued and the spotlight again was back on Randy. But Warner's eyes were on Clara. She just might be his ticket past the unwanted fame his step-mother brought him. Perhaps, she could help him with the career he'd worked so hard to build.

CHAPTER 6

*C*lara was more than impressed with how the song turned out. Love Song. Oh, what Carrie Underwood could do to that song, she thought as she slipped her guitar into its case as the next act took the stage.

"You totally upstaged me, you know." Randy gave her a light shove with his elbow.

"Excuse me." She shoved back with a laugh. "This was your show. I borrowed one song."

"And it was amazing."

"It was, wasn't it?"

Randy growled. "Why thank you, Randy, for your kind compliment. Bless your heart," he mimicked.

"Thank you," she grunted back. "Maybe someone heard it— the right someone."

"That's the name of this game isn't it? Sing till the right someone hears it."

. . .

WARNER LOOKED AS PETRIFIED AS HE HAD WHEN SHE'D LEFT HIM with her family at the beginning of the set. That wasn't usual. The Keller family usually embraced everyone.

This made her worry.

What did they see in him?

"You were amazing as always!" Darcy raced around the table and gave her a hard hug, which was followed by her mother, father, and the rest of the family.

Warner stood, but backed up against the wall.

He didn't understand family. She could see it in the fear in his eyes. Well that was going to have to change. You couldn't be part of her life and not enjoy family.

There it was again. Why the hell did she care?

Christian pulled up another chair for Clara to sit next to him and Randy planted himself at the end of the table next to Spencer.

"So what did you think?" She brushed up against Warner with her shoulder.

"You guys sound great together."

"Yeah, but what did you think about your song?"

"Oh," he nodded nervously. "I couldn't have imagined it sounding better than that."

"It was good. Wasn't it?" She grinned until her cheeks hurt.

The waitress brought her Blue Moon in a glass with an orange adorning the side. She squeezed the orange into the beer and then dropped it inside.

She looked at Warner. "What are you drinking?"

"Pepsi."

"Want a beer? I'll order you one."

"No," he quickly answered. "I'm good. Thanks."

CLARA'S FAMILY WAS THERE TO SUPPORT HER. THEY TALKED AND drank until their glasses had run dry. Then they all kissed her and left in small groups until she was there with only her brothers, Darcy, and Warner.

"Your family didn't want to stay for the other sets?"

Clara shrugged. "They come for me. They always have."

Warner nodded slowly, picked up his Pepsi, and sucked down what was left of the cola and melted ice.

"I suppose you need to be going too," he said. "Thanks for singing the song. It certainly gave me some hope that maybe with your voice it would sell."

Clara reached her hand out and covered his. "I was kinda hoping that you and I could spend some time getting to know each other."

WARNER FELT HIS HEART RACING, IN HIS THROAT.

This woman knew exactly who he was and wanted to still spend time with him? Dear Lord, she must be out of her mind.

At some point she would figure out that spending time with him was only going to ruin the career that she was building—which had immense potential.

He cleared his throat, hoping to shove his heart back in his chest. "What did you have in mind?"

"Dinner. I don't eat before I perform and I'm starving."

Her easiness was quickly wearing off on him. "I could certainly go for a bite to eat," he said as she took his hand and stood.

"I know the perfect place."

CLARA'S JEEP WAS A MUCH NICER RIDE THAN WARNER'S BEAT UP pickup. He was pleasantly surprised to find that she had installed an XM radio and was listening to the Highway. They had some great things in common.

Great music was one of those things.

He watched the sights of Nashville from his window and then turned his head toward her. "So how come your entire family comes to hear you perform even when you're not the lead performer."

"We're family. We support each other."

She could be talking another language. He didn't understand family support at all.

She gave him a glance before focusing on the road. "I'm sorry about your dad."

He let out a breath and shifted his eyes back out the window. "Thanks."

"I hope you don't mind. I looked you up on the internet."

He shrugged. "I wouldn't expect you to not want to know about the guy who stalked you from the street."

She laughed easily. He envied that about her.

"Patricia Little is a thorn in your side, isn't she?"

"She does her best to tear me down."

Clara's lips pursed and she gripped the steering wheel tighter. "I don't understand that. I mean even when my parents were divorced they were civil to each other. In fact, I think they were better friends."

"Your parents aren't divorced now?"

"No" Her lip curled up in a look of confusion and then settled into a smile. "Oh, I sometimes forget that the whole world does not know about the Keller family."

"What does that mean?"

Clara guided the Jeep into the parking lot, parked, and killed the engine. She grinned wide.

"Ever eat here?"

"Steve's Barbecue Pit and Beer?"

"Another Keller staple."

He let the tension slide off his shoulders and now he was smiling. "You introduce me to your entire family and now bring me to a Keller hang out? And here I thought you were just going to steal my song."

The smile on her lips disappeared. "You thought I was going to steal your song?"

"Hey, my track record with beautiful women isn't very good. Most women in my life either abandoned me, tried to ruin me, or have used me to meet someone in Nashville to kick start their career."

"First of all, thank you for thinking I'm beautiful." She smiled. "But I don't work that way—I don't use people."

"I see that." There was a gnawing sense of guilt rising in his chest. "Before we go inside and you somehow convince me to spill to you, I just want to thank you for taking the time. I've spent the past few years with people already having formulated opinions on me because of some...well some..."

"She doesn't influence my decisions."

Warner swallowed hard. "That means a lot."

Clara reached across the Jeep and rested her hand on his thigh. "You're good people, Warner Wright. I've been surrounded by good people my whole life and I know one when I see one." She patted his leg and then retracted her hand. "C'mon. I'm starving and you're right," she said as she opened the door. "I'm going to make you spill your story."

As Clara climbed out of the truck Warner took in a deep breath. Fate must have stepped in and given him a shove. How else could he explain the fact that he'd met the only person in Nashville without an agenda of their own?

CHAPTER 7

*T*he restaurant was packed with patrons. The fragrant smell of barbeque and stale beer permeated Warner's senses. The hostess guided them to a table for two in the corner. Clara took her seat before he could even attempt the gentlemanly maneuver of pulling her chair out for her.

Warner sat across from her and looked over the extensive menu.

"I'll order if it's okay," she offered.

He closed the menu and nodded.

Clara ordered their meal and then leaned forward on her arms when the waitress left and looked Warner in the eyes.

"Okay, so I know your dad was once married to Patricia Little. Tell me who you really are."

There shouldn't be any reason to be nervous. Clara didn't make him nervous. He just hated talking about his life. Really, who wanted a thirty-year-old sob story?

"Born and raised in Memphis. In fact, I could see the back yard of Graceland from my bedroom window." He started to bounce his leg under the table, which he did when he was nervous so he willed himself to stop. "I suppose that was where I got the bug. How can you not live that close to Graceland and feel the spirit of rock and roll, gospel, and the true roots of music as we know it?"

There was an enormous smile on her lips. "That has got to be the most awesome thing I've ever heard."

This girl didn't get out too much. "I lived there until I was ten." His heart rate kicked up a notch and his knee was bouncing again. "That was a year after my mom took off and my dad met Patty."

"Patty?"

"Patricia Little."

"Oh," she sighed the word and he knew it was out of pity.

"They were married a few months after my parents were divorced, or so he said they were. I don't have any proof that they actually did get divorced." He waved his hand in the air as if to discount what he'd said. "Anyway he married Patty and we moved just outside Nashville."

"Your mom just up and left you?"

"Yep." His mouth had gone dry. Where was that waitress with their pitcher of beer? "One day she and dad were fighting, then she told him she hated that she'd gotten pregnant with me and he'd made her stick around. So he told her she didn't have to and she left."

Clara reached across the table and took his hand. "Warner, I'm so sorry."

Her thumb caressed the top of his hand. He liked the comfort of the gesture, but he itched to pull back. But he refrained.

"Not everyone gets a perfect family. I'm okay with that."

She gave his hand a squeeze and released him. Warner quickly pulled his hand back.

"Anyway, we settled in. Dad was working two jobs and Patty was making friends." He cleared his throat. "They were married two years by the time he realized she'd run off with all the money and left him with nothing but bills—and heartache."

Warner cleared his throat. "The only thing he had to offer me was a life insurance policy."

Clara covered her mouth with her hands. "Warner..."

"He did what he thought was right. He didn't consider that suicide was the one factor that would void the policy."

"Warner, that's horrible."

The waitress set the pitcher of beer down in front of them and Clara poured them each a glass. Warner picked up his glass quickly and took a long pull.

"My mom was gone. Dad was dead. And Patty took off and eventually got involved with a very married Harley Oxbury."

"What happened to you?"

People usually wanted to hear about the fall of the OX. Clara was the first person to ever ask what happened to him after his father's death.

"My maternal grandmother took me in until I was eighteen."

"So you had a good home?"

"I had a roof over my head and food on the table. You might imagine that my mother hadn't wanted to be a mother, my grandmother wasn't very fond of her role either."

He could see the pain Clara was feeling in her eyes. People pitied him. Some felt he deserved it. But he could see that Clara genuinely felt pain for him.

"So what did you do when you were old enough to move on your own?"

Pride swelled in his chest. "Well, I got a job. It was a crappy job, but I was a janitor at a junior college. I had room and board and an opportunity to get an associate's degree. So I have an associate's degree in business. Then I got into the University of Tennessee and moved to Knoxville. I had a full ride and I got a degree in music."

Clara's eyes were bright again and she smiled. "That's wonderful."

"I know. Who would have thought?"

"You did. And that's all that matters."

Oh, she was a gem. "It was great until I got a teaching job and Patricia Little had lost everything again. She was trying to mend her reputation. She'd married a record exec and she went about using her influence to convince the school board that I was harmful to students."

"That's not fair," Clara sat back in her seat. "Why do people do that to others?"

"Jealousy."

"It's ridiculous."

"I think so too." He took a sip of his beer. "The downfall has been this stupid TV show of hers. She's been married four times now and she has slammed the good name of each of her ex-stepchildren."

"She's a monster. I don't think I'll watch that show anymore."

He laughed. "I don't hold that against you."

"She's my least favorite one on the show, if that helps."

"A little." He smiled as the waitress set down one of the biggest meals he'd ever seen in front of them. "Dear Lord, who are you expecting?"

"Crazy isn't it? We'll have plenty for lunch tomorrow."

"I think this is as much as I eat all week."

Clara shook her head. "Nah, we're going to get these songs sold and you're going to start eating like a king."

Yep, it was fate that put him in the path of Clara Keller. They may never sell a single song, but he felt better than he had in a very long time.

CHAPTER 8

*W*arner wasn't sure when he'd eaten so much. His stomach felt as though it might burst.

He tried to recline in the Jeep, but it was no use. He was happy in his heart and miserable in his body at the moment.

Clara pulled up outside of The Stage and parked her Jeep. "Looks like things are slowing down tonight," she said.

"It is funny that this town could be so busy on a Wednesday night. If you think about it, it's slow, but anywhere else a Wednesday night crowd would have all gone home."

She laughed. "You're right." She rested her head against her seat and looked at him. "I had a really nice time tonight. Thank you for sharing it with me."

"Clara, I haven't shared my story with very many people. Most people already have an opinion of me."

"Well then they are stupid. How can anyone take that no good woman's word for it?"

"Because she's on TV."

She blew out a breath. "I'm going to continue to form my own opinions."

He felt it coming. He needed to kiss her. He needed to be

more to this woman than just the guy who showed up begging her to sing his songs. He...

He had no time to make a move before she came across the cab and planted her lips against his.

A groan, or maybe it was a moan, came from his throat when he realized what was happening.

It wasn't just a gentle brush of the lips kiss. No, this woman was planting a hot, passionate kiss on him and he was thinking too hard. How was it that he needed to remind himself to pull her to him—which he did. His mind worked over time when she pushed against him and ran her fingers in his hair, which was too long.

No—he wasn't supposed to be thinking about his hair.

God, she was killing him.

CLARA COULDN'T HELP HERSELF. HER BROTHERS AND RANDY WERE right—Warner Wright was just her type.

He had a sob story, but who didn't.

He had eyes of blue she could drown in and sandy hair she could bury her fingers in.

His mouth was soft and gentle, but when he'd finally started to kiss her—oh Lord, she could faint.

It was completely understood, in her own mind at least, that she might have just screwed up everything. Warner might think she's just out to use him, but she couldn't stop what she was doing.

Oh, she would stop. She wasn't the kind of woman to let things go too far, she wasn't ready yet.

When she finally did pull back they were both breathless. "I couldn't help myself," she said. Certainly she wasn't going to say she was sorry.

"I had just been thinking about doing that myself."

She laughed at that. "Good."

"This changes things a bit, doesn't it?"

She sat back in her seat. "How about we agree that we don't let it?"

He nodded. "Agreed."

"In fact, meet me at the theater tomorrow around lunch and we'll finish off these leftovers."

"You have to rehearse?"

"I have auditions."

"You're auditioning for another show?"

She shook her head. "No. I'm directing it.

He smiled. "I think that is extremely cool."

Clara chuckled. "Would you like to audition?"

"No."

She sighed. Oh, her heart was gone. "I'll see you tomorrow then."

He opened the door. "Maybe tomorrow you can tell me your story."

"My story?"

"Yeah, I was extremely sure that your parents were married by the way they acted tonight."

"They are married."

He was smiling. "You said they were divorced."

Clara nodded. "I suppose that does need some clarification, huh?"

"Tomorrow." He stepped out of the Jeep. "Goodnight."

Clara watched him walk toward his beat up truck. She sure hoped he wouldn't be disappointed if they didn't sell his songs. He had a lot of faith in her that she didn't have.

Sure, she could belt out a tune and she loved the work she did in the theater. But singing had just been a love—a passion. It was never supposed to be relied on.

She'd do her best and she only hoped her best was enough.

CHAPTER 9

*C*lara pulled into the driveway and put her Jeep in park. Her presence didn't seem to bother her brother any. Christian continued to kiss his girlfriend Victoria goodbye at her car.

She laughed as she climbed from the Jeep and reached in for the carry out bag of barbeque. Christian was happy and that meant a lot to her. But it didn't mean she wasn't going to do all she could to razz him about it.

Victoria raised a hand in a wave as she climbed into her car and Clara walked up the front steps to the house her Aunt still owned and she now occupied.

Christian limped toward her.

"Why don't you go home with her?" Clara asked as he neared her.

"She's a very, very good girl. We've been discussing our future and it seems that perhaps sleeping in the same bed just might work out for her...soon."

Clara laughed. "She's in her mid-twenties, works with athletes, and is a virgin?"

Christian's face hardened. "I didn't say that. I said she was a very good girl. Sometimes that means changing how you think about things and taking another path."

Clara nodded slowly. "She's not going to sleep with you."

He huffed out a breath and walked past her into the house. "You know, Mom would appreciate and approve of us waiting until we're married."

"You're getting married?"

"I'm thinking about it."

That did something funny to Clara's stomach. She followed Christian into the kitchen and touched his shoulder. "Is that why you're having a house built and you're sleeping in my spare room?"

"I'm not going to be a ball player much longer. In fact, have you seen me even play in a year? No, because I'm benched and can't even walk the freaking plates."

"Chris…"

"I'm washed up and I never got the chance to even be someone."

"That's not true."

Christian shook his head. "Listen, I don't have business sense like Ed. I don't have talent like you. I could play ball and now I can't."

She didn't like when he got like this. If she kept pushing, he'd fall down a pit of depression, and she'd seen him do that too much in the past year. Victoria was the one person who kept him from hitting rock bottom.

"I'm happy for the two of you. I think she'd make a wonderful wife."

His face softened. "I do too."

"I bet you'd have real cute kids too."

This time he smiled wide. "Her sister and Dave—our pitcher," he said looking at her for confirmation that she did indeed know who he was talking about. "They have the damn cutest kids I've ever seen."

Clara laughed. "Christian Keller, I think you're a goner."

"Yeah, I think I am."

Clara moved past him to the refrigerator. She made a space for the bag of barbeque and pulled out a bottle of water. She twisted off the cap as she heard footsteps moving up the back stairs toward the kitchen.

"Hey, Tyler."

"Hey." He stood before her jean clad and barefoot with no shirt. She noticed he'd gotten a new tattoo on his arm. The welts were still fresh.

"New ink?"

"Yeah. Kinda felt like I needed it."

She smiled. It was the infinity symbol that she had on her wrist and each of her brothers and Darcy had too.

"I like it," she said before taking another sip of her water.

Tyler nodded as he rested against the wall, his thumbs tucked into the front pockets of his jeans.

"Listen, I'm sorry I wasn't there tonight to hear you sing. I was told it was amazing—as usual."

It had been a few months, but Clara saw the unmistakable pain in Tyler's eyes. Ed, her oldest brother, had met a woman and they were going to get married. Who would have ever thought that Ed's fiancée was the sister Tyler had never known about?

Clara moved toward him. "This family is too tight for you to feel pushed out. You can't go on forever blaming your mother for giving up Darcy and not telling you about her."

Tyler nodded. "I know. It's just going to take some time. I love her. I really do. She's been nothing but genuine and straight forward with me. I'm honored to have her as my sister. But it hurts." He shifted a look toward Christian, who must have already had this conversation with him. "I think I'm going to take some time and see the world."

"See the world?"

"Yeah. Take a year off of school. See the world. Put my life into perspective, and then come back, graduate, and take my seat at BBH."

"What does your dad think about this?"

Tyler bit down on his lip. "He's not crazy about the idea. But to be honest, I think Spencer has a better head for business."

Clara moved in, wrapped her arms around him, and gave him a squeeze. "Perhaps you do need to find yourself. But don't forget where you came from and who your family is. We all love you."

"If I wasn't half Keller, I don't think I could do this and know it would be okay."

She knew well enough that statement was true.

Clara stepped back. "Well, I'm beat and I have auditions tomorrow and a show on Friday. I'm heading to bed."

"So that guy, the one who wants you to sing his song…"

She turned back toward Tyler. "Yeah, what about him?"

"His mom is Patricia Little?"

"Ex-stepmother."

Tyler nodded. "Is he a good guy?"

She smiled. "The best."

"Good. I don't want to come back from seeing the world and have to beat the crap out of some loser."

She shook her head. "Yep, I have two brothers and two cousins who would kill the first man to break my heart."

"You know it."

"I'm a lucky girl." She gave them a wave and headed up the stairs. Something told her Warner Wright wasn't a threat.

Patricia Little on the other hand—what could she do to Clara if she hated Warner so much?

WARNER WAS RESTLESS. HE'D TRIED TO GO TO BED. HE'D TRIED warm milk. Nothing was working. Clara Keller had him stirred up.

He turned on the small lamp on the end table in his rink-adink apartment and sat down at his electronic piano keyboard. Warner wasn't a bad neighbor, so he plugged in his headphones and set his fingers on the keys.

A melody formed. He closed his eyes and played. This was Clara Keller's melody. It fit her. It was smooth and easy, but there was an underlying contrast of sharpness to her. She didn't take crap and she didn't dish it out. She cared, deeply cared about people and family. And damn if she didn't carry herself with more grace than a princess when wearing jeans and cowboy boots.

She was tattooed, but he assumed just the one. She was brass and not mad. She was his fate.

The notes took a sour turn at that point and he tore off the headphones.

Record the demo.

Sell the songs.

Get the career he'd been working so hard for.

That was it. The list was short and sweet. Adding feelings for a woman were not part of the plan.

He looked at his watch. Three-fifteen in the freaking morning and he was wide awake and stirred up. Lord help him. It was going to be a long night.

CHAPTER 10

*C*lara was sitting on the front steps of the theater talking on her cell phone when Warner parked his truck. She must have been having quite a conversation too, because her hands were in her hair, her head was down, and she didn't see him until he'd walked up on her.

She gave him a nod to acknowledge him and then looked back down.

Warner turned so it wouldn't appear as though he were just listening in.

"I have shows all weekend. It's closing weekend," she said. "I don't know how I'm going to squeeze that in…Yeah, I know it's great. I didn't ask for this did I?" She blew out a breath. "I know… I know. Okay, I'll talk to him and I'll get back to you."

Warner turned around as Clara stood, the phone still pressed to her ear. "Randy, I'll make it work. Just book it and I'll be there."

With her final words she pushed the button to finish the phone call.

"Sorry," she said on a sigh and then took a step toward him.

"I didn't mean to interrupt." His breath was thick in his lungs as she neared him. "Everything okay?"

"Never better, actually. We'll talk about it later." She stepped up to him and pressed a kiss to his lips.

He hadn't expected that. He'd convinced himself that the kiss they'd shared the night before was a fluke.

Clara pulled back, but left her body leaned into him. "I got done with auditions early. Let's go get something to eat."

The urge to push the strand of stray hair from her eyes won over his better judgment. "I thought we were having leftovers."

She laughed as she wrapped her arms around his neck. "It seems as though I forgot to put a huge sign on it that said not to eat it. My brother and cousin finished it off after I went to bed last night."

"You live with your brother and cousin?"

She leaned back and gazed at him. "C'mon, hot dogs at Frank's and I'll tell you about my parents, the rotating house, and the phone call."

She nipped his lips one more time with a kiss.

"Let me get my things." She turned and went back inside.

Warner let the intimacy settle in his gut. Something was heavy on her mind and it had to do with Randy. But she still wanted to be with him and that made the situation lighter. This wasn't what he'd bargained for when he chased her down three days ago. But the comfort he felt when he was around her was worth the crash that he knew was coming.

The door to the theater opened again and Clara walked down the steps, her sunglasses shielding her dark brown eyes. "Why don't you drive?"

"Are you sure? Your Jeep is much nicer than my truck."

She interlaced her arm through his. "I'm sure."

"And where am I headed?" he asked as he pulled open the creaky door to his truck.

"Riverside Building. I thought it would be fun to see if Ed and Darcy would like to have lunch with us."

"They both work in the building?"

She smiled. "Yes. I have a lot of family that works in the building."

He nodded and walked around the front of the truck then climbed in next to her.

"What does Darcy do there?"

"She is Ed's assistant."

He started the truck and eased out onto the street. "So, you were going to tell me about your parents."

"Did you stay up all night wondering about that?"

He cleared his throat. Well, he'd been up all night thinking about her, but he wasn't going to share that information.

"You said parents, rotating house, and phone call. Your choice in which order you start your story."

She grinned and cranked down the window. Clara sucked in a deep breath and closed her eyes. "God it's a pretty day today."

"A bit too hot don't you think?"

"Nah. It'll only be a few months and we'll be complaining that it's too cold."

He chuckled as he turned at the light. "True enough. Okay, so talk."

She turned toward him and pulled her legs up under her on the bench seat.

"My parents were high school sweethearts. They married young and started a family. My mom put my dad through college to get his teaching degree. Somewhere between working two jobs, having three kids, and my dad taking a long time to secure a really good job, their marriage broke apart and they got divorced."

"How old were you?"

"Six."

He cringed. "That's pretty little."

She nodded. "I can't say I knew too much about it. One day Dad moved out, but he was always around." She smiled. "To tell you the truth I think we saw him more when he didn't live with us."

Clara readjusted her legs. "Mom remarried soon after their divorce was final. She married my dad's best friend."

"Ouch."

"Yep. But he was a good guy. Perhaps a little lonely considering he married his best friend's ex-wife and then had an affair and left my mom when he got his mistress pregnant."

Warner laughed aloud. "Oh, you do have some drama in your life."

"That would sound like it." She chuckled. "Anyway, Matt, my step-dad, eventually left my mom, married this other woman and I think they have four kids now."

"Wow, that's a lot."

She let out a sigh. "I don't think so." Then she turned her head to him. "Do you really think so?"

He felt the heat crawl up the back of his neck. Was she really asking his opinion on family size? What did he know about family dynamics? "Any kids are a lot."

Her shoulders dropped and the curve of her lips turned downward. Oh, he'd messed up that answer.

"Anyway," she waved her hand through the air as if to reject his answer. "Matt left the day before Mom found out she had breast cancer."

"That's insensitive."

Her smile was back. "You'd think, but no one knew about this. She didn't tell anyone. In fact, she decided to go through a double mastectomy alone, that way no one would worry about her."

Warner shifted his glance to her and then back to the road. "That's not some little in and out surgery."

"I know, right?" Clara adjusted in the seat again. "She was out of sorts. That's all I can say. But, my Uncle Curtis was on call at the hospital that day and he saw her being wheeled into surgery. He called Dad and he was by her side the moment she woke up. It was the beginning of our happily ever after as a family."

"So they got back together that day and she beat cancer?" he asked as he headed toward the huge building that graced the Nashville skyline.

"Well she did beat cancer, but it took a little time for them to patch things up. Dad was engaged after all."

Warner was grinning. Her drama had nothing on his, but when she told her tale he realized even the most put together of families was dysfunctional.

"Your dad, he dumped his fiancée?"

"Oh, no. He's not that kind of man. He'd made a commitment to Kathy and he was going to see it through."

"But he was still in love with your mother."

Clara turned her head and eased against the seat. "I didn't say he loved my mother."

"You didn't have to."

Her smile widened. "He had never stopped loving her. What a sap." She laughed. "Anyway, he married Kathy and mom refused to go to the wedding. Instead she headed to Mexico and met some man."

"Reality TV has nothing on this relationship."

She winced at that and continued, "He married Kathy, but she came to her senses before they'd even been married twelve hours. She told him she'd made a mistake and wanted out. She had a friend in the travel industry who took his ticket to Hawaii, where they were going to spend their honeymoon, and she had his ticket fixed so he'd go to Mexico instead."

"His new wife sent him after his ex-wife?"

"Yes she did."

"That's gutsy."

"I guess when you realize you made a mistake, you might as well suck it up and make the best of it, right?"

That one hit home. "Yeah."

"Kathy is married now with three kids and she's happy as far as I know. Dad went to Mexico, got Mom, and they came home and got married—again."

"What about the man in Mexico?"

"I don't know about him. Just some guy who friended her. They never mentioned him much."

Warner could understand that.

Clara pointed to the entrance to the parking garage and Warner headed that way. "Okay, this house you live in."

Clara adjusted in her seat again, tucking her other leg under her and shaking out the one she'd been sitting on.

"The house." She took a breath. "Keep up, okay?" She laughed. "My Aunt Arianna, who owns the theater, owns the house. When she left for Broadway she let my Aunt Regan live there, after she'd returned from living in Hawaii."

He nodded. "Okay."

"When Dad needed somewhere to live he moved in with Aunt Regan."

He nodded again. So far so good—he was keeping up.

"Regan married Zach and moved out. Dad moved back home with Mom. Then Zach's company took over the property and managed it with tenants. Uncle John then moved into the basement and Aunt Arianna came back from New York."

He knew he was smiling like a fool, but he was enjoying this. "Got it."

"Aunt Arianna and Uncle John got married and built a new house and my brother Christian moved in, upstairs. When Darcy moved to Nashville she lived in the basement until she and Ed moved in together. There is a story there too but we'll save that one."

"O-kay," he drawled out as he found an open space that would accommodate his truck.

"Let's see. So now Christian lives upstairs, but he's building a house for him and his soon to be fiancée, but don't tell her because I don't think she knows he's going to ask her."

Warner chuckled. "I promise."

"And my cousin Tyler lives downstairs, for now." Her face lost its glow.

"Is he going somewhere?"

"He just needs to find himself. It all has to do with that Darcy and Ed story. I'll tell you later." She opened the door to the truck. "I'm hungry. Let's go see what Ed and Darcy are up to."

CHAPTER 11

The moment the elevator opened to the floor of Benson, Benson, and Hart, Warner shook his head. "Your brother works here?"

Clara gave him a sideways glance. "You know the company?"

"I used to be a courier. I've been in this office a few times."

She smiled wide. "Zach Benson. Does the name ring a bell?"

"If I remember right, he's the CEO."

"Uncle Zach."

Warner sucked in a breath. This girl had a lot of connections. "At least I know when I fall flat on my face in the music industry, maybe I can have you put in a good word for me to sweep up construction sites."

"I know many men who have started there." She walked down the hall toward Ed, who was walking toward her. "And there is one of those men."

"He worked on site?"

"Everyone should start at the bottom, don't you agree?"

He'd never given it any thought, but she was right. And that was where he was at, wasn't it? The very, very bottom.

The smile on Ed's face was wide as he walked toward his sister. "What are you doing here?" He embraced her tightly.

"We thought you and Darcy might be available for a hot dog down stairs."

He nodded and gave a look at Warner before holding out his hand to him. "Warner, it's nice to see you."

"Thanks. You too."

Ed looked back at his sister. "Darcy and Regan are shopping. They said they were couch shopping, but something tells me they'll be looking at wedding dresses."

"That is so exciting, don't you think?"

"I don't care what she wears. I just want to get married. But I know she wants to wait until Tyler feels better about it."

Warner saw Clara's expression change. "He'll be fine in time."

Ed nodded. "I know he will." He sucked in a breath and pushed back his shoulders. "Okay. Let me close my door and I would love to have lunch with you."

THE PLAZA ON THE RIVER FRONT WAS BUSTLING WITH PEOPLE ON their lunch hour. Warner was familiar with the hot dog cart they were walking toward. Frank had set him up many times over the years when he didn't have two dimes to rub together.

"Warner!" Frank shouted from the folding chair next to the cart. His daughter helped customers, but turned to smile.

Warner held out his hand to Frank, who shook it with great vigor. This warmed another cold space in Warner's chest. "Frank, how are you?"

"Living the good life." He looked at Ed and Clara. "You know this guy?" He smiled at Ed who held his hand out to Frank and he shook it.

"How are you, Frank?"

"Never better." He narrowed his eyes at Clara. "Which one are you?"

"I'm Clara. I'm Ed's sister."

Frank nodded his head. "I should have known," he said with a smile. "C'mon, my Pearl will get you all set up."

They ordered their lunches and Ed quickly paid. Warner didn't like that, but inside he'd admit he was more than grateful to have saved a few bucks. He thanked Ed and followed them to a concrete picnic table down by the river.

"This is great," Ed said taking a bite out of his hot dog. "I was afraid Mary Ellen was going to feed me a salad. She's trying to get Zach to watch what he's eating."

Clara turned to Warner. "Mary Ellen is Zach's assistant."

He nodded and took his first bit of his lunch.

"So what are you two doing?" Ed asked.

"Getting to know each other. I was filling Warner in on Mom and Dad's marriages."

Ed laughed. "Well one thing you'll never be lacking is a good Keller story. We are one very eclectic bunch."

"I think that's awesome," Warner said trying to choke down his bite. "My family story is short and sweet. I think it's cool that you all have each other."

"She told you the Kellers are mostly adopted, right? So we represent, literally, the whole world at the dining room table."

"She didn't mention that yet. I don't think."

Clara sipped her soda. "My dad is adopted. He was born in Puerto Rico and became a Keller at the age of seven. My aunts, Regan and Arianna, are blood sisters, but were adopted when they were very little. Uncle Curtis is the only blood Keller to my grandparents, and he married Simone who is French." She giggled. "And when you meet my grandmother, whom you'll love, she speaks with a German accent accentuated with Southern charm."

"And yet you're all so close."

"I don't suppose you can find a tighter knit family."

Warner already knew that—longed for it. Again that nagging

reminder beat in his chest. He needed Clara's voice. She was going to be his ticket. This little relationship they were building was a mistake, and he knew it. It would be best if he got what he needed and got out before Clara got hurt. He wouldn't be able to live with himself if something happened to her because of him.

CHAPTER 12

*W*arner watched Clara type a text message on her phone. Something was eating at her, but she'd yet to bring it up. One thing he'd learned in his life was to leave things alone. When she was ready to tell him, she would. But he couldn't help but feel that whatever was bothering her had to do with him.

He eased his beat up pickup truck into the parking space in front of the theater and Clara finally looked up.

"You don't have your music and guitar with you do you?" she asked.

Warner winced. "Wouldn't be a real musician if I didn't, right?"

She nodded. "Do you have time to come in and work?"

Warner twisted in his seat to look at her. "Work? On music?"

She let out a sigh. "Listen, Randy got this gig for us. You and me."

"Us?"

"Yeah. But it's closing night at the theater."

"Oh." He saw the dilemma now. His stupid thought on her being the voice to sell his music was backfiring because she had a

BERNADETTE MARIE

life. Everyone had a life, and usually it didn't include him or his music.

"He said Lionel Perry heard your song the other night and contacted Randy."

"Lionel Perry?" His voice rose in pitch. "Lionel Perry as in the same man who has discovered some of the biggest names in this town? That Lionel Perry?"

"Yes."

Warner ran his hand over his hair. "Wow. He heard my song?"

"You're going to have to do this on your own, though."

That phrase didn't settle with him—nor did it surprise him. "Right." He let out a deep breath. "Can't we reschedule?"

She shook her head. "C'mon, isn't this what you've always wanted? Someone to want to hear your music? Warner, you're more than just the words on paper. You have some great talent."

"You've never heard me."

Her smile was back and lit in her eyes. "YouTube."

Warner bit down on his lip. "You're not just saying that, are you?"

"I'm not just saying that." She reached her hand to his cheek. "You have to stop letting others get into your head."

He knew that, but it certainly was engrained in him "So you can't make it, but you're going to help prepare?"

Clara dropped her hand to his and interlaced their fingers. "Yes, I'm going to help you. Isn't this what you want? To perform your music for someone who wants to hear you?"

It was what he'd wanted more than everything. In fact until she'd said it out loud, he'd given up on wanting to perform and had settled to selling his music if the opportunity came along.

"I do want that."

"Well, c'mon then. Let's practice."

. . .

70

The theater was still set up for West Side Story. Clara pulled two chairs to the center of the stage and then retrieved her guitar from backstage.

Warner looked around the streetscape and thought of Clara standing on the fire escape singing down to her Tony. It occurred to him that there were only four shows left and he'd heard her sing, but he hadn't seen her perform. Perhaps he'd try to secure tickets for the show. And it was moments like that he wished he'd had a mother who'd like to accompany her son to the theater. Well, he swallowed the lump that had formed in his throat, he didn't have that so there was no reason to even let that get under his skin.

Clara returned with her guitar and sat down across from him. "Okay, handsome, let's make some music."

There wasn't much to her picking up the tunes he'd had tucked away in his head. She could read his scribble and adlib with the best. They'd run through one song, and on the second round she'd harmonize against him.

He'd never felt so alive.

They were genius together. The theater filled with their sound. He recorded each song on his iPhone and each one sounded better than the one before.

This could happen. This could work. He'd been right. Clara Keller could be his ticket.

The moment overtook him as she shuffled the music on the stand before her. Warner rose to his feet, walked to her, and pulled her to her feet. Each of them gripped the necks of their guitars in one hand. He slid his other hand around the back of her neck and pulled her to him into a kiss that should have melted his shoes to the stage.

His tongue sought out hers and a moan escaped her throat. Colors danced behind his eyelids and his heart pounded in his chest harder than the vibrations from sitting too close to the speakers at a rock concert. No matter what happened with his

BERNADETTE MARIE

music, he had to keep this woman. Nothing had ever made him feel as alive and as whole as this woman did.

His lips were warm and his mouth so inviting. She had to focus on holding tightly to the guitar so that it wouldn't fall to the ground.

Warner's fingers worked through her hair, and she raised her free hand to his chest, gripping his shirt in her fingers.

It was then, during the bliss of the kiss, when she heard the distinct sound of the theater lights being turned off.

Her eyes flew open and she clung to Warner, a scream was caught in her throat and threatened to choke her.

"Hello!" Warner called out.

Clara's hands shook as she gripped him tighter.

"Hello?" He called again.

"Clara? Are you in there?" John's voice called from the back of the stage.

"Uncle John, we're here."

A smaller light illuminating the back stage turned on and she could see him standing near the door.

"Sorry, kiddo. I thought you guys left. It got quiet." He took a step toward the stage. "I didn't mean to scare you."

Her hands were still gripping the front of Warner's shirt and her other hand had such a grip on the guitar that the frets were cutting into her fingers.

"I'm okay," she said, but her voice shook.

Warner looked down at her. "Are you sure you're okay? You're shaking like a leaf."

"I'm fine." She took a step back. "I said I was fine."

She let out a long breath and tried to steady herself. Her palms were sweaty and her hands still shook as she tried to gather the music off the stand as Warner tucked his guitar into its case.

John walked to her and placed his hand on her back. She winced and that bothered her.

"Honey, you okay?"

"I'm fine. You just startled me, that's all."

"I know. You haven't been this jumpy in years."

He was trying to keep her calm, but standing on that same stage with darkness enveloping, it brought back too many memories.

"Do you need a ride home?" John asked.

"I have my Jeep."

"Is Christian home?"

Clara shrugged. "I don't know." She sucked in a breath. "I'll be okay. I'm fine." She pushed her shoulders back. "I can lock up. You can go."

John shook his head. "Give me your guitar. I'll put it away and you two go out the front. I'll wait until you're out."

She wasn't going to argue. Clara handed him the instrument and started off the stage.

CHAPTER 13

Warner watched her walking away from him. He exchanged glances with John, who gave him a simple nod and then headed back stage.

Warner picked up his case and hurried after her.

She was walking at an ungodly pace, but he finally caught up with her when she crossed through the front door. But the last thing he expected was to have her turn into his arms and sob against his chest.

"Hey," he said as softly as he could, but he'd been nearly bowled over by her falling into him. "It's okay."

She sobbed into his shirt. This was a first. He'd never had a woman do this. Usually he'd been the cause of their tears, not the comfort.

Warner ran his hand over her hair and waited for her to either cry out all her tears or give up. He wasn't sure which had happened, but it took about five more minutes.

When Clara raised her head and began wiping at the tears that lingered on her cheeks, she shook her head. "I'm so sorry. That was so unnecessary. You didn't need to see that side of me."

"I'm not sure what I saw." He gripped his hand around the

handle of his guitar case a little firmer. "Did you just get startled?"

Clara looked at the ground and then back up at him. "I had a bad experience in there when the lights went off. That just took me off guard."

He could feel the heat rise under his skin, as if his blood were beginning to boil. He reached out for her. "Did someone hurt you?"

She was gathering her thoughts and biting her lip. Warner knew he'd felt heart break a million times in his life, but standing there waiting for her to tell him that someone hurt her—it was killing him.

"I just want to go home."

He wanted to shake the story out of her. How could someone have had that kind of reaction to something and then not want to talk about it?

Maybe she just didn't want to talk to him.

"You're really in no shape to drive. Let me give you a ride."

She took a breath, and he was sure she was going to argue, instead she clasped his hand. "I'd like that. Thank you."

THE DRIVE WAS QUIET AND CLARA FOUGHT WITHIN HERSELF TO gain composure. There was no reason for her to have gotten that worked up over something as silly as John turning off the lights. But she couldn't help it. There were just some events in your life that formed you into who you would become. The night she stood on that stage and the lights went out when she was thirteen would haunt her forever.

"Can I come in?" Warner asked and she snapped up her head. He'd parked in front of her house and she hadn't even noticed.

The lights were on upstairs which meant Christian was home. She'd be okay, but when she turned her head and saw Warner looking at her, the tears started again.

"Are you sure you want to come in and sit with an emotional baby?"

"Baby? Something set you off like this and you think I think you're a baby? Something tells me I'm a much bigger baby than you are."

That made her chuckle. "I think I would like you to come in."

Warner gave her a nod and jumped out of the truck. Clara wiped away her newly fallen tears and opened her door. Warner was right there with his hand out to help her down.

She easily slid into his arms as she climbed out of the truck.

He held her and she cried again. This was stupid, she thought. These emotions hadn't surfaced in years.

Warner didn't say a word. He held her tightly, right there on the sidewalk until she could compose herself.

"You ready to go inside?"

Clara nodded and hand in hand they started up the front steps. The moment she was in the house, Christian, sounding like a team of horses, hurried down the stairs and stopped abruptly when he saw Warner.

"Hey," he said, as if to cover up the grin still plastered on his face.

Clara felt a smile form as she batted back the last of her tears. He'd been coming down for gossip and hadn't expected her to have brought Warner into the house.

When Christian looked at her his smiled faded and he moved to her. "Hey, what's wrong?"

She felt Warner step back as Christian moved in.

"I just had a startle at the theater. John turned off the lights while we were practicing on stage…" another sob broke free.

Warner let go of her hand as Christian pulled her to him. "It's over, sweetheart. Long, long, over."

"I know. This is stupid."

Christian smoothed his hand over her hair as she rested her cheek against his chest.

"It's not stupid. That was a part of you and you have every right to be frightened. And all of this is fresh in your head because of Darcy being around, and its okay."

"This isn't Darcy's fault," she argued.

"No, but it's in our heads." He gave her a squeeze. "Listen, go up and take a hot shower. I'll make you some tea and a sandwich." He pushed her back so he could look at her. "It was over that night. He'll never hurt another Keller, ever."

She gave him a nod.

"I'll let you be. I'll see you tomorrow, okay?" Warner stood, now closer to the door.

Clara turned. "You don't have to go. Please stay." She reached her hand to him and he grasped it.

"Are you sure? You seem to be in very good hands."

Clara moved from her brother to this man who in less than a week had become more important to her than anyone else. She wrapped her arms around him and rested her head to his chest. "Stay. I'll be back down soon." She kissed him on the cheek and headed upstairs.

CHAPTER 14

$\mathcal{W}$arner watched her disappear and then focused on her brother, whose eyes were focused on him.

"Sounds like she had quite a night," Christian said still keeping a steady eye on Warner.

"She's pretty frightened."

"And John just turned off the lights and she got like this?"

Warner nodded. "That's about it. I don't know what set her into this, but that triggered it."

Christian took a step closer to him. "You don't know why she's like this and yet you're this calm around her?"

"Hey, man. She needed a shoulder to cry on, a set of arms to hold her. She'll tell me in her own time."

Christian took a step back and the corner of his mouth curled up. "You're one of those very patient men aren't you?"

"I don't know about that. I just know this isn't any of my business."

"C'mon," he started for the kitchen. "I'm going to make it your business."

Warner followed reluctantly. Finding out about someone's demons was a big step to take. But Clara knew he had this stupid connection to Patricia Little and she was still sticking her neck out for him.

"Have a seat. Can I offer you anything?" Christian pulled a mug from the cupboard.

"I'm fine," Warner said as he sat down at the kitchen table.

"Crap, I can't remember which one of these is supposed to make her calm." Christian pulled down the two boxes of tea he'd been staring at in the cupboard.

Warner wrenched his neck to see what he had in his hand. "The black tea will keep her awake. The green tea is supposed to be more soothing."

Christian turned his head and lifted a brow. "You know this?"

"One of my many many jobs was as an assistant to this antique dealer. She was a tea freak. You have only so many cups of tea thrown at you before you get it right."

"If she's throwing hot tea at you, I hope you didn't work for her for long."

"You do what you have to do to pay rent and eat."

Christian nodded and pulled a green tea packet out of the box. He then filled the tea pot with water and set it on the stove before pulling out a chair and sitting across from Warner.

"Just so you know, my sister doesn't spook at just anything. It's not like she's afraid of the dark—usually."

Warner nodded. "She doesn't come across as a woman who lets things bother her."

"My aunt was involved with this man once. We didn't even know him. We were really little and they lived in Hawaii." Christian drummed his fingers on the table. "They were engaged, having a baby, starting a new life."

Warner watched him and the lines around his lips began to deepen.

"He decided to marry someone else, for wealth. As if the S.O.B. wasn't wealthy enough." He shook his head. "Anyway, he decided the best thing to do would be to kill my aunt and the baby."

Warner felt the blood drain from his head. "Are you kidding me?"

Christian shook his head. "He beat her and left her to die, still pregnant." He sucked in a breath. "Well, they both survived. My aunt gave up the baby for adoption so that he couldn't get to her and she went on to marry and have two great sons."

"They caught this guy? Locked him up?"

"No." Christian closed his eyes for a moment. "The bastard left the country with his new wife."

"Coward."

Christian chuckled. "He surfaced a few years later and then again when Clara was about thirteen."

Warner felt his heart rate kick up. This was where it became real to him. This bastard had something to do with Clara, and already he could feel every muscle in his body tense.

"Why would he come back?"

Christian sat back in his chair. "He was now in the knowledge that the baby my aunt was carrying had survived. I think it was all a power trip, because he didn't want that baby. But his wife divorced him, left him broke. He was seeking revenge."

"He came after her?"

"He came after the whole family." Christian leaned in and rested his arms on the table. "My other aunt was remodeling the theater with John. Their first production was going to be Annie and Clara was going to have the lead. They were told to meet there, but he was there."

Christian's eyes had glazed over and Warner realized he dug his own fingertips into his thigh waiting for Clara's part in this story.

Christian blew out a breath. "He turned off the lights. Grabbed Clara and locked her in the props closet."

Warner felt his temperature rise with anger.

Christian drummed his fingers again. "Then he set fire to the building."

"Oh, God!" Warner wanted to find this man and kill him himself. Who did that to a young girl?

"My aunts got her out of the closet. She inhaled a lot of smoke though." He ran his fingers through his hair and went back to tapping them on the table. "They were able to get through the theater and out to the lobby before he grabbed them again. But somehow Regan got the gun out of Arianna's purse and she shot him." A smile crept across Christian's lips. A smile of pride. "They got out, he died in the fire."

"No wonder she freaked out. That is horrible."

"She went through a few years of counseling over it. Dad being in education knew she had to. He saw too many kids messed up by events in their lives. It's never been an issue to her. She knew the man wasn't after her. Clara just got in the way. But she still had nightmares."

"You said something about this all coming back because of Darcy. Ed's Darcy?"

Christian smiled and scratched the growth on his chin. "Darcy is the baby."

"The baby your aunt gave up for adoption?"

"Yep. Funny how things happen, huh?"

Warner gave some thought to the Keller family story. "And since your dad and your aunts are all adopted then Darcy and Ed aren't related at all."

"That's how it goes."

Warner let out a little laugh as the whistle on the tea pot sounded.

Christian stood and poured the water into the mug. "Clara was fine until Darcy came into the picture and the story was brought up again. She doesn't blame Darcy, it just surfaced memories."

"I understand that." Warner couldn't hear an old OX song

without thinking of the moment he found his father dead. He shook off the thought. "She's a strong woman. I don't suppose there is anything that could take her down."

"You two gossiping like little girls makes me wonder about how strong you big men are though." They both looked up to see Clara standing in the doorway.

Her hair was wet, and much darker than normal. She wore a pair of yoga pants and a tank top. She obviously had skipped the bra and that had Warner looking away and down at the table.

Clara sat down at the table and Christian pushed the mug toward her.

"Thanks."

"No problem." Christian walked around her and gave her a kiss on the head. "I'm going to head upstairs. Tori is supposed to Skype."

"Where is she?"

"L.A." He stood up straight and held his hand out to Warner who shook it. "Thanks for taking care of my girl."

He looked at Clara who smiled. "My pleasure."

Christian headed upstairs leaving Warner and Clara in awkward silence.

"I assume you know why I'm a chicken in the dark."

He reached for her hand. "I don't think that way. You have every right to have been frightened."

"It was a long time ago. It upsets me more when I get upset over it."

He understood that emotion. "It looks to me that everyone takes good care of you though when you need it."

She smiled. "Yeah. The Kellers work that way."

"I've already seen it quite a bit in less than a week." He ran his thumb over her knuckles. "It'll never go away. You just learn to deal with the situation that frightened you."

Clara narrowed her eyes. "You're talking about your dad, aren't you?"

"I found him."

"Warner…"

He sat back and shrugged. "He ran the car in the garage. I sometimes wonder if he meant to take me with him in his forever journey."

"Why?"

"Because I was home asleep in my bed."

Clara covered her mouth. "That's horrible."

"It is what it is. And if I never get a record deal or sell one song, I'll know I'm a survivor. So are you."

"I guess us kind should stick together, huh?" She moved in closer to him.

Warner rested his forehead against hers. "You're willing to risk it all over some slob like me?"

"You may not have been raised a Keller, but something tells me you have the same kind of fight in your blood."

He grinned. "I like that."

"Stay with me, Warner. Just hold me all night."

"Are you sure?"

"Yes. Let's both sleep our demons away wrapped in each other's arms. Nothing more—just comfort."

He knew he shouldn't accept the invitation, but he couldn't help it. This had gone far beyond needing her voice. He needed her.

CHAPTER 15

$\mathcal{T}$he private world beyond Clara's door told Warner
exactly who she really was, and it brought a grin to his
lips.

Her bed was unmade. The girly rose covered comforter was
bunched up at the bottom of the bed as though she had been too
hot to sleep with it. There were miscellaneous clothes strung
over the back of a chair in the corner of the room and a pile of
shoes making their exit from the closet by way of potential
avalanche.

A guitar sat in the corner as well as a keyboard. Sheets of
music lay on the floor next to them in a pile.

Clara was carefree and this proved it to him. Nothing was too
important and Warner liked that. Living with his grandmother
that hadn't been the case; a perfectly organized and tidy house
was more important than anything, including the happiness of
her grandson.

But Warner knew a creative mind. He had one too and his
apartment didn't look much different. Though, had he brought
her to his house, he'd have been running amuck trying to pick up
everything. Clara embraced her individuality, he decided,

because she didn't seem to worry what he might think. And he thought the mess was lovely.

Clara turned to him and smiled. "You're eyeballing my mess."

"I am not."

"Yes you are. You think I'm a pig. My mother always warned me that someday…"

"I didn't take you to my house, did I?" He laughed. "Your room looks fine."

"I have too much to do to worry about duvets and pillow shams."

"Do whats?"

Now she laughed. "Nothing." She moved in closer to him. "I know this seems silly. And I'd understand if you'd want to go."

"Why would I want to go?"

"Because I don't have sex with men I've just met."

Warner took a step back to distance himself from her. "You said sleep over and that was all. Clara, I'm not the kind of man…"

She moved into him again. "I know you're not. That's why I asked you to stay." She rose up on her toes and pressed a kiss to his lips.

Being trusted wasn't something he dealt with a lot. He usually hid from any reason to be trusted. There was always the chance he'd let someone down.

Clara picked up an old T-shirt and a pair of shorts off the pile on the chair. "I'm going to go change. I could find something for you to sleep in if you'd like. Christian should have…"

"No," he interrupted thinking that borrowing her brother's pajama bottoms was certainly crossing the line. "The boxers I have on are new, no holes." He laughed. "If you're comfortable that will work for me."

Clara grinned and her cheeks flushed pink. She nodded and headed to the bathroom with her pajamas.

When the door had closed he went about getting undressed. Maybe if he were in bed, covered up, it would ease her.

He toed off his boots and pulled off his socks, stuffing them into the boots. He shimmied out of his jeans and pulled off his T-shirt then folded them nicely and set them on the floor in a tidy pile.

Warner quickly fixed the sheets on the bed and climbed in as the bathroom door opened.

As awkward as she looked trying to be normal, he knew Clara Keller wasn't used to bringing men home.

She turned off the light and climbed into the bed next to him. She turned to face him. "Thank you for staying with me. John turning off the lights shouldn't have set me off like that."

Warner caressed her face. "You went though some serious trauma. I don't blame you for freaking out. I don't think you ever get over that moment when your life flashes before your eyes."

Clara smiled and rested her head against his chest. "You're right. You never do."

He pulled her closer to him. She rested her head against his chest and he held her. A week ago he didn't know what he was doing with his life. Now he wondered if music was his calling at all? Or had it just been the force that brought him to Clara Keller? He kissed the top of her head.

This was what he wanted more than to hear his song on the radio. How could his dreams have changed so quickly?

THE NEXT MORNING WARNER DROVE CLARA BACK TO THE THEATER and went on his way home. He had the urge to clean house because after holding Clara all night in his arms, he wanted to make that a normal occurrence.

As Warner pulled up in front of the small building which looked like a house with four small apartments, he saw a black BMW pull away. He parked in the spot the car had occupied, turned off the overworked engine, and climbed out of the truck.

Warner rubbed his eyes under his sunglasses. He was tired. He shouldn't be, he'd gotten a full night's sleep for the first time in weeks. At least his current unemployment offered him time for a nap.

He climbed the steps to the second level of the quad-plex and walked to the dull red door with the number two nailed to it. A bright yellow piece of paper hung there adhered with a piece of tape.

Warner thumbed through his keys until he found the right one. He jiggled it in the lock and finally pushed open the door. As he walked through he tore off the paper and carried it inside.

For a moment he stood there and then kicked the door shut behind him. What a horrible little hell he'd created for himself in that little apartment.

Pizza boxes and two liter bottles littered the table where he wrote music. His keyboard had no less than three stale mugs of coffee balanced on it. As if he could afford for one of those to spill—he'd paid an outrageous fortune for that damn thing. And did he have a cat? No, but it smelled like he did.

He threw down the piece of paper he'd collected from the door along with his keys onto the cluttered coffee table and let out a long breath. No napping. He needed to clean this place up.

THREE HOURS LATER WARNER FELL ONTO THE COUCH, KICKED HIS feet up, and closed his eyes. Six bags of trash had been taken to the dumpster. Four baskets of laundry had been carried to his truck so he could make a trip to the Laundromat.

His cupboards were now filled with clean dishes and he'd thrown out the rotten strawberries in his refrigerator and made a grocery list. Other than condiments, he had no food.

Rubbing his forehead with the back of his hand he laughed at himself. He was a slob. Clara's cluttered little bedroom was a haven compared to the hell hole he'd been living in. But maybe that needed to change.

Warner tapped his hand against his leg and a beat generated at his fingertips. The hell I've created...that would need to change.

He sat up and tapped the same beat on the coffee table. The hell we've created...it was time for a change.

The words danced in his head and beat now tapped his foot.

He stood and walked over to the newly dusted keyboard and began the workings of the song that now played in his head.

CHAPTER 16

*C*lara sat at the kitchen table and bit into the sandwich she'd made for dinner. It was nearly nine o'clock and she'd been calling Warner since she'd left the theater. He'd never answered.

She was setting herself up for disappointment. He had a wanderer's soul and she was just a stop on his route to wherever he was going to land.

The house was too quiet. Tyler was gone and the basement was void of everything but the furniture that stayed. Christian was at Tori's. It seemed as though she'd decided he was worth having over at night. And now Clara sat alone in her kitchen with a piece of bologna between bread and she was calling it dinner time. She was pathetic.

Well, it was only one night. She knew she shouldn't feel bad for herself. Tomorrow night would start the final run of West Side Story. Her days as Maria were numbered. And then there was the gig Randy had set up for them, though it was going to have to be all Warner now. There was no way she could commit to performing with him.

As she bit into her sandwich there was a pounding on the front door. She yelped as she bit down on her cheek.

Who could possibly be at the door this late?

The pounding continued and Clara quickly stood, hurried to the cupboard, and reached for her gun. She'd hated Christian leaving it there, but now she was glad it was in reach.

"Clara, are you home?" She heard Warner's voice call out.

Her adrenaline had kicked in and she laid the gun back on the shelf. Her hand was shaky and even holding it in her hand wasn't safe.

She took a deep breath and hurried to the door.

As she pulled open the door she narrowed her eyes on him. He was a wreck. Were those the same clothes he'd had on when he left her off at the theater?

"What are you doing?"

His eyes were open and bright. "You have to listen to this." He moved past her with his guitar in his hand, not even in its case.

Warner propped his foot up on the coffee table, raked his fingers through his already mussed up hair, and then he began to play.

Clara smiled as Warner dove into the song. The dark cords, his deep voice, the haunting lyrics of a love on the mend. The man was a musical genius.

The song and his voice echoed through the house which only moments earlier had been so quiet. This was where he'd been all day she realized. The creative mind had shut off from the world and this masterpiece had been written.

As the last chord of the song resonated through the air he finally looked up at her. His eyes were wide and he was waiting for her approval.

"You wrote that today didn't you?" She asked.

He only nodded, his foot still propped up on the table. His guitar still balanced on his knee.

"Warner Wright, I think you're a genius."

"You do?"

Clara nodded. "That was one of the most amazing songs I've ever heard."

His eyes darkened and narrowed. "Let's record it."

Clara laughed. "Now?"

"Yeah. I have my computer in the truck." He set his foot down and held the guitar by its neck.

"You don't even know what time it is, do you?"

Warner scratched the back of his neck and then pulled his cell phone from his pocket. He winced. "Eww, sorry. I didn't realize it was this late." He tapped his finger on the screen of his phone and scrolled through the list of missed calls. "I didn't even know you called me."

"Obviously." Clara crossed. "You need a shower."

He looked down at himself. "God, I am a slob. But my apartment is clean." A line crept between his brows. "But all my clothes are dirty and in the back of my truck. I forgot to go to the Laundromat."

Clara covered her mouth to keep from bursting into laughter. This certainly was going to take some getting used to. The creative mind, she'd learned, was very disorganized.

"You have your laundry with you?"

He nodded.

"Go get it. I have a washer and dryer."

"Right. Thanks." He propped the guitar up against the couch, set his phone on the table, and fished his keys from his pocket. A folded up piece of yellow paper came with the keys and he set it on the table. Obviously it had been what he'd written the song on.

Clara watched him as he hurried out to his truck.

Oh, they had pegged her—her brothers and Darcy. Warner Wright was just her type.

CHAPTER 17

*A*s Warner carried in his laundry Clara buzzed around the kitchen.

"That's the last one. I'll pay you back for the use of the washer."

She set a plate down on the table with a sandwich on it. "Eat. I'll bet you haven't done that all day either."

His stomach growled as if on cue. "You're right. I cleaned my apartment and wrote. As productive as I was—I wasn't very productive at all."

"Sit. I'm going to start that laundry and you're going to relax."

Warner sat down and picked up the sandwich. Bologna? Did people in real houses really eat that? He'd never been one for the strange meat, but it was cheap enough for him.

He bit into the sandwich and began to feel the drain of the day settle into his muscles.

The noise from the other room of Clara loading the wash machine twisted guilt in his belly. But the realization of the moment kicked in. Never in his life had a woman taken care of him. Clara had known him a week and there she was making him sandwiches, listening to his songs, and washing his clothes.

He rubbed the stubble on his chin. His grandmother never even washed his clothes. That had been his job.

No woman had ever listened to his songs with that same spark in their eye either.

Clara hadn't been mad that he hadn't answered her. It was as if she understood that he'd completely lost track of time—of everything.

She walked around the wall from the laundry room with one of his shirts. "You're not going to actually wear this shirt again are you?"

She held up a T-shirt he'd had since—well he wasn't sure since when. "Of course."

Clara shook her head. "I assume it used to be black. It is a green-gray color now and full of holes. I'm throwing this away."

Warner bit into his sandwich again. And just like that, the woman of his dreams was throwing away his bachelorhood.

The bite of his bologna lodged in his throat with his thought. He coughed to clear the blockage.

She was taking over his life and his clothes. Already she'd taken over his mind which was leading to his heart.

As she walked away with the shirt wadded up in her hand, he cleared his throat. He'd officially tumbled in love with her. Damn —that was fast.

WHEN WARNER WAS FINISHED WITH HIS SANDWICH HE WALKED HIS plate to the sink. There were no other dishes in the sink. Clara's bedroom, her most intimate space was cluttered with her individuality, but her home was tidy.

The dishwasher was running a load of dishes already. Now what?

He let out a chuckle. You wash the damn thing, he thought.

Warner opened the cupboard under the sink and took out the bottle of dish soap and a sponge. When the plate was clean, he held it over the sink and looked around for a towel. One hung from the handle of the oven. Sunday was stitched on it.

As he pulled it down and dried his dish he had to think hard. It wasn't really Sunday was it? No...no he knew that for a fact.

Clara walked into the kitchen and stopped. She smiled easily and he liked that.

"Did you wash that plate? You could have just set it in the sink."

"That didn't seem right. I've been cleaning all day. Maybe I'm still in the cleaning mood."

"If you say so." She pulled out a chair from around the kitchen table and sat down. "I have a show tomorrow night."

Warner tucked the towel back over the handle of the oven and looked at Clara for direction as where to put the plate. She pointed to a cupboard.

He had to admit there was a bit of alarm in his chest when he noticed a pink handled pistol sitting there.

Hoping he was discreet enough, he put the plate on the stack, closed the door quickly, and sat down across from Clara.

"Last four shows, right?"

"Yeah. Friday night. Matinee on Saturday. Saturday night and Sunday night."

Warner nodded. "And the gig on Sunday."

"I won't be there."

"I know." He swallowed hard. "I'm trying to still wrap my head around that."

She leaned in over her arms which rested on the table. "I want you to come and see me. My family is coming tomorrow night. I'd like you to be there."

Heat rose in his body. The feeling was uncomfortable enough, but when he hadn't showered all day it wasn't good either. "And when you say your whole family you don't just mean your mom and dad."

"You catch on quick." She laughed and sat back in her chair.

"In fact, I think Darcy's dad is here from Florida with a lady friend and he's coming too."

"Of course, because the Keller family isn't big enough."

That made her laugh hard. "Right."

Was this a test? Would he pass if he refused? What was he thinking? He didn't want to refuse. He wanted to be there.

"I'd love to come. Where do I buy a ticket?"

Clara's eyes softened and so did her body. "God you are cute." She stood up and walked to him. She pressed a kiss to his forehead. "One will be at the box office waiting for you."

"Thank you."

"Now, you march upstairs and get a shower. Christian has some lounge pants on the dryer you could wear until we get your clothes clean."

"Yes, ma'am."

She cupped his chin in her hands and looked down at him. "And then I want to show you what I set up for us."

Huh, he couldn't even begin to imagine where that was leading, but anywhere with her was where he wanted to be.

CHAPTER 18

*C*lara was the perfect hostess. She'd handed Warner a warm towel and a toiletry kit with a toothbrush and a razor.

"The snarky man in me wants to ask if you have overnight guests a lot. But the gentleman in me knows that's not why you have these." He held up the sealed bag she'd handed him.

"Christian throws those in his suitcase when he travels. He can't remember to pack those items when he's leaving, so the bags are easy. And he can't remember to bring them home, so they are disposable."

"Nice."

"I'll be downstairs." She handed him a pair of lounge pants and a T-shirt, then walked out of the room.

By the time he made it downstairs, after his shower—and shave—the kitchen table was filled with his clean clothes. They were neatly folded into like piles and he could hear Clara starting the washer again.

She smiled when she saw him. "You look better."

"Thanks."

"No disrespect. I've seen Randy get that way too. He gets to working on songs and never surfaces for days."

That twisted in his gut. But he thought to her brother's expressions when he'd made a comment about Clara having a relationship with the man. Obviously they just worked together and there was no attraction. Warner was wise enough to be grateful for that.

"Are you ready to see what I set up?" Clara opened the door to the basement.

"Sure." He walked across the cold kitchen floor toward her. She turned on the light to the stairs and headed to the basement.

At the end of the stairs there was another kitchen which he knew led to the apartment where her cousin had lived.

Clara turned on more lights and led him down the hall to the bedroom.

"John helped me put this together today," she said as she turned on the light.

The bedroom had heavy moving blankets hung up on the walls. The bed had been disassembled and sat propped up against the wall. Two stools sat in the center of the room. A music stand sat in front of them, a towel draped over it.

"You built a recording studio?"

She smiled at him. "I don't have any equipment, but…"

"I do," he interrupted. "I mean I have what we need." His voice had risen in pitch. A surge of adrenaline had bolted though him when he realized what she had done.

Sure, it was simple, in a room that wasn't being used. But it was the thought. She had done this for him—for them. She'd included her family.

"I'm free tomorrow until two," she added. "We could start recording…"

He couldn't keep it in any longer. Warner grabbed her arm and pulled her to him with a thud.

She let out a grunt, but his mouth was on hers quickly.

There was no protest. Not that he'd expected any.

Clara wrapped her arms around his neck and deepened the kiss he had started.

Warner moved her until she was pressed up against the mattress which was leaning up against the wall.

The air in the room was growing thick. His was becoming heavy, the kiss more intense, his need—uncontrollable.

"Warner," her voice was heavy on the air—thick with lust.

He moaned something that urged her to continue as he moved his lips to her neck.

"Let's go upstairs." She swallowed hard beneath his lips. "My room." Her breath was being gulped in as she pulled her fingers through his hair. "I have protection up there."

He was hearing her words, but he wasn't believing them. Then again he was sure as hell going to take her up on it. Thank goodness she was practical too.

Warner pressed his over willing body close to her and she held him tight. "Are you sure about that?"

"Uh-huh."

She escaped from beneath him and took his hand, pulling his out of the room and back up the stairs. They were a mess of tangled limbs as they tried to hurry through the kitchen and the living room, their mouths still attached.

They tried to skirt in front of the couch, but her foot caught the edge of the coffee table and she yelped a curse and fell to the couch below.

"Did you hurt yourself?"

She pulled her leg up, crossing her knees to look and laughed. "Yes."

"I'm so sorry."

"I'm not. Give me a second and I'll be fine. It just hurts."

Warner nodded and watched her rub the pain from her foot. He looked down at the table where he'd dropped his keys and his cell phone. The yellow piece of paper he'd written the song on lay there crumbled up. He'd pulled it off his door and it was the closest thing he'd had when he needed to write on something. But now the front of it was face up.

EVIC was all he could see.

He quickly reached for it and pulled it open.

"Son-of-a-bitch!" He tried to unwrinkle the message.

"What's wrong?"

"I'm evicted."

"Evicted?" Clara jumped to her feet, obviously forgetting about the pain she had been in. "Why would they evict you?"

He looked the paper over. "Because they sold the damn building." He read down further. "Oh no she didn't!"

He reached for his phone.

"What are you talking about?" Clara took the paper out of his hand. "They sold to the P. M. L. group?"

He dialed the number and put it to his ear. "Patricia Morgan Little."

"Oh!"

The phone rang in his ear and then her nasty and annoying voice mail took over the call. He pushed the end button and nearly threw down the phone—of course he had a better mind about it. He didn't have three hundred dollars to replace a phone. And to top it all off, the bitch had kicked him out of his house.

"Warner, maybe I can have Zach look into this."

"Why? This is how she works. She's just a nasty…"

"Why would she do this to you?"

"Because this is how she works. She's had four step children and she does crap like this all the time to all of us. And none of us are even involved in her life anymore."

Clara shook her head. "I don't understand."

"What is she going to talk about on that stupid show of hers if she doesn't have one of us to belittle and upset? This is a shock factor maneuver. She's doing this to hurt us and then her ratings go up. She's all about being the nasty bitch on that show and they pay her handsomely for it. She doesn't care what people think of her."

"Then you move in here."

"Clara, you're not making any sense."

She fisted her hands on her hips and stood there glaring at him. "I'm making perfect sense. You move in here with me."

"I'm sure your family would think differently of that."

Her hands came up and she huffed out a breath. "I'm offering you a perfectly good place to live. No one can evict you from here. And you could record your music and get your songs out there. Isn't that what you want?" She turned to walk out of the room and turned right back around. "I'll tell you what. You can live here until you have a fancy tour bus and then you can live there. But I'm trying to help you out. I won't just have someone I love thrown out on the streets and treated like this. That woman can go to hell for all I care."

He was sure the blood had drained from his head. That was his cue to sit down and he did.

"You're just going to sit there?" She slapped her hands down to her sides. "Lord, you're a pain."

She moved to walk past him and he grabbed her hand. "Do you even know what you've just said?"

"I said move in here. Patricia Little doesn't affect me. I can have her…"

"No. That's not what I'm talking about."

"Now you're not making sense."

He loosened his grip. "Why do you want me here?"

"You're important to me."

He stood up and looked down into her dark eyes. "This has nothing to do with her now." He reached his hand to her cheek and caressed her soft skin. "Tell me again what you said before. About me being thrown out."

"Oh." Her cheek grew warm under the tips of his fingers. "I said I wouldn't have anyone I loved be treated like this."

"Love?"

She let out a sigh. "Love."

"That is one hefty word."

"It sure is," she agreed. She moved in closer to him. "I don't just say it either."

"I've never had anyone say it to me at all."

"Never?" She pressed against him.

"Never."

Her lips moved to his neck. "I think that should change."

He swallowed hard. Was he ready for this? Why was he so nervous?

"Warner," she whispered in his ear.

"Huh?"

"I love you."

Okay, maybe he wasn't ready for the words. His heart rate kicked up harder than it had when she'd had her hands on him in the basement. His palms grew sweaty and his mouth had gone dry.

"Clara..."

"Shhh, don't say anything. I don't want you to repeat the words. Not yet." She gently pressed her lips to his. "Now, the offer stands."

"Me living here?"

"That one too." She took his hand and started toward the stairs. "We can discuss that in the morning. Patricia Little is not about to ruin what I was already working on."

"Oh." His voice cracked as Clara started up the stairs.

CHAPTER 19

*W*arner could have died right there in Clara's arms and been perfectly content with the life he'd lived. The memory of the night they'd shared filled his mind as he drove down the highway. Every night could be like that. The rest of his life could be like that.

The woman loved him.

What an amazing feeling to have someone want to be with you, he thought. It wasn't like he was some sad virgin. He'd had a lot of sexual experience, but this was the first time someone had actually been in love with him and it made all the difference in the world.

All he could do was pray he didn't screw it up.

Warner pulled up in front of his apartment building. Already one of the units was moving out. This was the first time he'd ever been grateful that he didn't have anything.

"Hey, Warner. Thanks for nothing, pal," his neighbor yelled down to him.

Warner wracked his brain for the man's name, but was coming up empty. "Beg pardon?"

"That mom of yours. Nice how I have to move out of my own house."

"Ex-step-mother. I have nothing to do with this. I'm homeless now too."

"Whatever." The man went back into his apartment.

Warner let himself into his apartment and shut the door. Patricia probably had a hidden camera somewhere and was sitting back laughing her ass off at his expense. Not only was he homeless but a half-dozen people now hated him just because of her. He rubbed his hand over the back of his neck. At least she couldn't touch Clara. Nothing would happen to her.

Clara's house was owned by her aunt and so was the theater. All of that was off limits. Patricia Little was almost out of ammunition.

But he didn't like how he felt about moving in with her. Warner had never had a woman say she loved him. He was quite sure he wasn't going to react well if she said it again.

He sat down in his chair and put his hands on his knees.

She'd not only said she loved him, but offered him her house and had freely given him her body. He wiped the back of his hand over his forehead.

There was a lot of pressure on him now.

Oh, Patricia Little could buy up all of Nashville for all he cared. But he had to get signed. He had to sell his music. No, he had to sell himself.

Warner stood and paced the little living room. He was a decent performer. His relation to that stupid woman was all that ever held him back.

Clara was right. He needed a big tour bus—one he could live on. And she needed to live on it with him.

The blood in his veins coursed through him with a different rhythm. He was going to sell that music. He was going to let his voice be heard.

Take that P. M. L., he thought to himself. He had a woman to love now. Anything was possible.

Suddenly his mind was filled with the thoughts of giving Brad Paisley and Tim McGraw a run for their money. He couldn't wait to perform on Sunday. He was going to knock someone's socks off. There was always someone in the crowd.

∼

CLARA ARRIVED AT THE THEATER EARLY. HER STARBUCKS COFFEE was a venti and her sugar fix was in a bag.

"You're here early," Arianna said as Clara set her bag on the table in the office.

"Felt like getting a start to my day."

Her aunt watched her dissect her coffee cake, breaking it into four pieces and setting it out on a napkin.

"You and Warner spent the night together, didn't you?"

Clara felt the heat in her cheeks. "Why do you say that?"

"You have that satisfied look about you."

"Not what I want to talk to my aunt about."

Arianna laughed. "You're in your thirties. I get to talk to you like a woman."

Clara dropped her shoulders. "I love him. I have fallen madly in love with this guy who a week ago chased me down."

"You're a Keller. I've seen romance blossom quickly and all sorts of things happen."

That was true enough. Zach and Regan met when she fell in his lap on the bus. Curtis met Simone at Clara's father's wedding to Kathy and they had a weekend and ended up pregnant. Darcy and Ed met and were engaged within months. No one was going to be surprised that she'd fallen in love with the musical misfit.

"I asked him to move in with me." The moment she said it she realized she should have asked her aunt first.

Arianna nodded slowly. "With Tyler gone I guess the house is a little more quiet."

"Right. And Chris' house is almost done."

"Of course." Arianna's lips pursed. "John said you turned the bedroom in the basement into a recording studio?"

"Only for the moment. If you get a renter we take down the carpets." God, she'd really screwed up. She could see it in Arianna's eyes.

"Right. But for now you could record and try and sell his songs?"

"That's the plan." Clara lifted her mocha to her lips and took a big sip.

"You sounded really good the other night. You sure you don't have it in you to just be a performer?"

She choked on the flavor and her aunts words. "That wasn't the deal. I told him I'd help him."

"And Randy's been telling you for years that you have what it takes."

"Well, yeah…"

"And this guy has the talent to write anything."

Clara thought about the song he'd written just yesterday. The melody had played in her head all night long and she knew that together they could make it amazing.

She sipped her drink again. God, was this what she really wanted? She'd been performing since she was thirteen. There was a certain adrenaline that pumped through her when she performed. The other night when she performed Warner's song that feeling was even stronger.

"Think about it, Clara," her aunt said. "You've already decided not to take on any more roles right now. Maria was a great success for you, but you're too old for her now."

That hurt. But it was true. Her co-star who played Tony was only twenty.

Clara pulled a chair up to the table and sat down. Warner had been so gentle with her all night that she knew her heart would break if he ever left. She'd fallen for him hard and if she could have it her way she'd keep him forever.

But would he stay—especially if she changed her mind on performing?

Randy would be ecstatic. He'd wanted her to perform more than she had. But what happened if she got signed? What would happen if she didn't?

Oh, all of this was stupid. She took a bite out of her coffee cake. Clara Keller was perfectly happy singing backup for Randy, directing the shows at her aunt's theater, and recording demos for Warner so he could sell his songs.

As far as she was concerned she'd won the lottery. Not only did she have all these great things going for her, but the man she loved was at that moment packing up his life and moving in with her.

Enough crazy talk about her performing with intent to sign with a label—though that wasn't what Arianna had said, but it was what Clara had heard.

Clara finished her drink and popped the last of the coffee cake in her mouth. In a few hours she'd be Maria again and that was where her focus had to be.

But as she stood and tossed her bag and cup in the trash she did think that opening up for Blake Shelton would be an ideal job.

She shook her head. Lord, she'd lost her mind.

CHAPTER 20

*T*here hadn't been much left to pack into Warner's truck. He'd called in help from a friend to load his couch and bed. All it would cost him was a beer. That was easy enough. He had one more stop to make before he headed home to Clara.

Patty Little needed a word.

PATRICIA LITTLE'S EXCLUSIVE NEIGHBORHOOD WAS GATED. ENOUGH rage ran through Warner that he had considered ramming the gate with his truck.

A uniformed man stepped out of the small guards' house as Warner pulled up. He gave the beat up pickup truck full of used furniture a once over before walking to the window.

"Mornin', how can I help ya?"

Warner smiled kindly and said, "Patricia Little please."

The guard nodded slowly. "She expectin' you?"

"I assume at some point she is. The name is Warner Wright."

The guard nodded again and went back into the guards' house, lifted the receiver to a phone, and began to talk. He was just out of ear shot for Warner to hear him, but he knew he'd been given the go ahead. A moment later the gate swung open and Warner drove through on his way to the house of the Devil.

The house was beautiful. Warner's dad would have enjoyed the nice yard—had he not felt the need to end his life because the witch had run off with everything the man had.

A black Mercedes was parked in front of the house and Patricia's white Lexus was in the driveway.

Warner parked his ugly truck right in front of her house, big as day. Maybe someone would think she was slumming if they looked out their front window. After all, all that nasty furniture and boxes in the back of his truck it was possible some old, rich, woman would have a heart attack thinking the neighborhood was going down.

The doorbell ring was nearly as annoying and pompous as the house itself. Warner simply gritted his teeth, tucked his thumbs into his worn out—but clean—jeans, and rocked back on his heels as Patricia opened the front door.

"Warner, what a delight to see you."

"Really?" He fought the million curses running through his head. "So why'd you kick me out of my house?"

"Strictly business, honey. Come in. Come in."

There wasn't an opportunity to refuse. She turned and walked into the house only leaving the option to follow if he wanted to continue his conversation with her.

Warner shut the door behind him and kicked off his old boots. He hated being there. He hated the woman. So why did he always hear his father's voice nagging him to keep things clean for her and not make a mess.

When he caught up with Patricia she was in the kitchen pouring him a sweet tea and even balancing a sprig of mint on the side.

"Come. I have a guest you know."

Warner took the glass and followed her to the back porch. He could have thrown the glass against the wall. There sat Jordan Farr, owner of Master Records and the only man who hadn't ever completely laughed Warner out of his office.

Damn!

"Warner," Jordan said as he rose to his feet and extended his hand toward him. "It's nice to see you. Hasn't been but a few weeks has it?"

"Just a few, sir."

"Did you find someone to help you record those songs of yours?"

Warner shifted a glance toward Patricia who had a painted cherry red grin on her lips.

"I'm working on that," Warner said. He was sure Patricia already knew too much. No need to fuel her fire.

"Warner, sit, honey." Patricia pointed to a chair next to Jordan. "Jordan and I go way back, don't we sweetheart?"

"Sure do," Jordan confirmed and Warner's stomach churned.

Had she just called him sweetheart?

"So, Warner," Patricia tapped her long nails on the side of her glass, "what brings you by? You never visit me."

Oh, she was good at this. If Warner started in on her in front of Jordan then it would be Warner that looked like an idiot. If he pretended to act as if he'd stopped by to visit, he'd look like a fraud, especially if Jordan ever watched her show.

What he wanted was some answers. That apartment building held no real estate value, so why buy it up and kick everyone out? Seriously, there had to be some legal recourse, though no one in the building could have afforded that and she knew it.

Warner stood. "Mr. Farr, it was nice to see you again. I think I'll come back again sometime. But I really should be going."

He set his glass of tea on the coffee table and headed back into the house. As quickly as he could he slipped his feet back into his boots, but he wasn't fast enough. There was the witch standing before him with her arms folded.

"Too afraid to yell at me in front of a record producer?"

"Not worth killing my career to let you hear what's on my mind."

"Career? Oh, you don't have a career. What you do isn't called music. It's called crap and no one, not even your new little girlfriend can sing your crap."

He instinctively took a step toward her. "You leave her out of this."

"Do you think she's a threat to me? Honey, I could, and will, crush her career too. Do you really think the papers will be nice to her for her portrayal of Maria? I don't think so."

"Don't do that. She's perfect in that part. Don't go messing with her just because you hate me."

"She's too good for you, Warner. When will you realize that you're trash just like your momma and no good just like your daddy?"

He fisted his hands to his side. "I still can't seem to understand why you even care what I do with my life. I'm not your son."

"No, but it's so much fun making you pay for that horrible marriage to your daddy where I got nothing. He did everything for you and forgot all about me."

Warner let out a disgruntled laugh. "Forgot about you? If that had been the case I'm sure he wouldn't have found the need to end his life."

"It was for the best. I suppose it's just too bad you woke up." The fake smile on her lips was gone and hate and heat burned in her eyes.

The woman actually hated him that much she'd wish him death. All the more reason, Warner thought, she should just forget him.

He turned and walked through the door. "You kicked all of those people out of their homes just to spite me, didn't you?"

"Business is business. I'd rethink that performance you have this weekend too. I'm just not sure it'll go well for you."

The door slammed in his face and he stood there on the front porch alone.

How did she know everything about his life? This was ridiculous!

He meant nothing to her. She'd wished him dead and yet she did all she could, for the past eighteen years, to make his life a living hell.

Warner turned and hurried back to his truck. He climbed in and enjoyed the horrible noises the engine made in her quiet neighborhood.

I'd rethink that performance you have this weekend too. What could she possibly do? *Do you really think the papers will be nice to her for her portrayal of Maria?* That comment still sizzled under his skin. What was she planning? What could she possibly do to Clara?

The only way to stop her attack on Clara was to not be with Clara.

He slammed his hand against the steering wheel. That was exactly what Patricia wanted. If he left Clara over her asinine review then he'd have lost the woman of his dreams.

The air in the cab of the truck was suffocating him. He cranked down the window and tried to suck in as much fresh air as he could as he drove out of the gated community.

Something had to be done.

Arianna. He had to talk to Arianna. Maybe she could field the reviewers. He didn't want anything bad to happen to Clara because of him. And he certainly didn't want to lose her either.

But there really wasn't much of a choice.

CHAPTER 21

*C*lara affixed her wig and let it fall long over her shoulders. She then took the white ribbon and tied it with a bow atop of her head.

Her makeup was heavy and the hair, oh the hair would always make her laugh. But it transformed her into Maria and for the next two hours that would be who she was. Maria, the girl in love with Tony.

All day things had been running through her mind, one was the look in Warner's eyes when he'd stopped by for the key. Something was bothering him and it was bad enough he couldn't even talk to her about it.

She closed her eyes and inhaled deeply. She held onto the breath for a moment and then let it out slowly. There was no time to let a man work into her head. Well, not her man. There was about to be a rumble between the Jets and the Sharks and that's all she could worry about. As far as she was concerned, for the next two hours, Warner Wright didn't exist.

. . .

WARNER HAD STOOD OUTSIDE THE BUSTLING THEATER FOR NEARLY twenty minutes. He'd watched her family walk inside. All of them including, what he assumed, were her grandparents. If he walked away there would be an obvious hole in the row of seats, and she'd said there'd be a ticket waiting for him.

He rubbed the back of his neck and started up the steps to the theater doors. As he entered the lobby the lights dimmed and returned. This was a sign that the curtain was about to rise and he'd better get his butt in gear.

Warner approached the ticket window by the door. "I'm a guest of Clara Keller. Warner Wright."

The woman nodded and an enormous smile formed on her mouth. "Oh, good. You're here. She's been up here four times to see if you'd picked up your ticket."

His jaw tensed. He forced a smile and headed toward the theater. He'd more than likely stressed her out just by thinking he may not show. Patty was right, her reviews were going to be bad if her head wasn't in the game and it would be all his fault.

The usher walked him to the front row. He'd been right. Right in the middle of the front row, which was occupied by her entire family and some of the second row as well, was an empty seat.

It looked like he'd be spending his evening between Ed and Clara's mother. Certainly it wouldn't look good if he threw up right there, center stage, since his nerves were shot.

Everyone stood and let him through. Each of them said hello to him, by name and shook his hand. Darcy was, perhaps, the sincerest yet.

Ed's handshake was a bit firm. "I thought maybe you forgot."

"No. No. Just got tied up." He tried to smile as he said it.

Clara's father stuck his hand out and in front of her mother to shake his hand. "Good to see you, Warner."

"Thank you, sir," he said as he shook his hand.

"Carlos. I appreciate the manners, but call me Carlos."

"Yes, sir." Hell, he couldn't help himself. At least Carlos smiled.

Clara's mother, Madeline, pulled him in for a hug and kissed his cheek. "It's good to see you again. Clara hasn't stopped talking about you all week."

She sat down and Warner followed as the lights dimmed.

The first notes of the overture began to play from beneath the stage in front of him. That chill that he got when he was about to see any kind of live performance, washed over him.

He got his first glimpse of the man who would steal Clara's heart—Maria, he corrected himself—and prepared himself.

It seemed like forever before the curtain opened on the third scene and there was the woman who held his heart. She stood in a white dress, her hair much longer and darker than usual. A chuckle wanted to surface when her Tennessee accent had been converted.

His eyes were locked on her and she was fully into character. Her entire family was within feet of her, yet she focused beyond them all. She was Maria.

Soon Maria met Tony and sparks flew. Even Warner was hopeful for them. But eventually they were in each other's arms and their eyes gazed into the other's. His own heart began to beat faster. When Maria kissed Tony for the first time, Warner was much too aware that it was Clara kissing that man.

His palms sweated against the pant legs on his thighs and his muscles tensed. There was chemistry between them and everyone in that audience felt it. Couldn't they get to the point where they all died—quickly?

What if she liked kissing that man? What if she'd kissed him often, off stage?

It was all too much and it swam in his head as if he were drunk. She'd known that man much longer than she'd known him. If sparks were going to fly between them they would have. It was him she'd asked to sleep in her bed, whom she'd made love too, and who had just moved into her house and left one hell of a mess in his wake.

When the curtains finally closed and the lights came up for intermission, Warner took inventory of how he looked and how he felt.

He'd been very conscious that Carlos had had his eyes on him the whole time. But it was Madeline's kind smile that met his eyes first.

"Isn't she amazing? Just amazing?"

"Yes. She really is." He meant it too. Clara Keller was full of talent.

"You should have seen her here the first night they opened with Annie, after they rebuilt." Madeline placed her hand on her chest and batted her eyes which had grown moist. "Oh, just thinking about it still gets me misty."

The thought of a young Clara with a red curly wig made him smile. Acting was different than performing music. Clara had to step aside from her life and create another, even for a few hours. He could take his trusty guitar up on stage and play as though it were giving him the breath he breathed. But not once did it mean he had to kiss a woman on stage and pretend he liked it.

That image was going to stick with him and he needed to let it go. What good was a jealous boyfriend when you had the career first? Yeah, he knew what that meant. It meant he'd be kicked to the curb and she'd still be kissing men who for a few hours she called Tony.

CHAPTER 22

*W*arner excused himself and headed out to the lobby. Christian gave him a wave from across the room and he nodded in return. There was a small bar in the corner and Warner thought he certainly could use a drink. But would that look bad? What would her family think of that?

"Hey, Warner, what can I get ya?"

He looked up to see Ed and Darcy smiling back at him. To Ed's side was one of her uncles—he fished for a name—Curtis. He was married to the French aunt. It was all coming back to him very quickly.

Warner walked toward them. "I'll have whatever you're having." He thought then it wouldn't seem too strange.

"Another Bud," Ed said to the bartender.

"So what do you think of the show?" Curtis asked as the bartender handed him a bottle of beer.

"It's amazing. I haven't been involved in musical theater in years, but I can tell you this is a class act."

The smile on Curtis' face told him all he needed to know about how proud he was of Clara and her aunt. Warner knew enough about the industry to know he should be proud of them.

Ed handed him his beer. "Thanks."

"Here's to Clara." Ed lifted his beer up and they all tapped theirs to his.

It was then Warner noticed the man in the corner holding his cell phone at a peculiar angle. Just the right angle to take pictures. Then he recognized the man.

He swallowed hard. "Excuse me," he said to the Kellers as calmly as he could and walked to where the man was now furiously using his thumbs to type something into his phone.

"Why are you taking pictures of me?" he asked the man who continued to type away.

"Just a job, man. Just a job."

"Erase them."

"Already sent."

Warner wanted to sock the guy in the gut and throw the phone against the wall, but he was very aware that the entire Keller family was watching him.

"Are you snooping or writing her review?"

That had the man's head snapping up. "Just a job, man."

"So you've said. I hope your review is more eloquent than that. And her performance is top notch. And if you print otherwise I'll make sure there is rebuttal against it. Her money isn't worth you ruining the career of someone else."

The man made an obvious gesture to push send on whatever he'd been typing and then tucked the phone into his pocket. "Like I said, it's a job…"

Warner held his hand up to stop him and he noticed it shook with anger. "Get out of here before I have you removed."

The corner of the man's mouth curled upward as he gave Warner a curt nod and walked out of the lobby through the front doors.

Warner sucked in a breath and then took a long pull from his beer as Ed walked up to him.

"You okay?" He reached out and rested his hand on Warner's shoulder.

Warner quickly evaluated his situation. Ed could very likely take him down right there in the theater literally or he could take him down by telling Clara he was no good for her. But then again, Warner knew that already in his own heart and he was sure he'd mentioned it to Clara too. But the fact was he loved her and he wanted her safe and happy and successful. How was that supposed to happen with him around?

"Seriously, man, you're freaking me out." Ed withdrew his hand.

"I'm fine." He let out a breath. "My ex-stepmother has sent one of her many minions to write a bad review about Clara."

"Why?"

"Because she can and people will listen."

Ed took a drink from his beer and was obviously contemplating what Warner had just said. "Why is Clara a threat to her?"

"She's not. She just happens to be the woman I love so said ex-stepmother will do all she can to destroy that."

He saw the vein rise on Ed's temple. "Love? You've known her less than two weeks."

"Yeah. I know it sounds stupid."

"If you're busting his chops for that I'll punch you in the stomach, Ed Keller," Darcy walked up behind Ed. "Warner, what can we do to stop his review?"

"Nothing. Freedom of speech."

She nodded. "There are a lot of reviewers. Not all of them have been to the show." There was a shimmer in her eye and a sparkle to the smile that formed on her mouth. "Let's just see what we can offer Nashville in twenty-four hours."

She walked away and Warner shifted his gaze back to a mortified looking Ed.

"What is she planning?"

Ed shook his head. "Patricia Little just messed with the

Kellers. You don't mess with the Kellers or the people they love." Finally a smile broke from Ed and he reached for Warner's shoulder. "Hold on tight. Might be a bumpy ride."

FOR THE REST OF THE SHOW WARNER SAT BETWEEN ED AND Madeline trying his best to keep his body still like a small child enduring the theater. Truth was that he wondered how many others Patricia had sent.

When Clara wasn't on stage, Warner would quickly do a subtle scan of the audience to see if he could see anyone he might recognize. He didn't.

There was no reason for Patty to mess with Clara, or him for that fact, except her disdain for him pushed her ratings and gave her a bigger paycheck. Maybe he needed a reality show.

The thought nearly made him laugh it was so funny, and the laugh would have been very out of place. It had come right as Tony was shot in the back.

He'd waited all night for this moment and now it was here. No more kissing, until tomorrow, but now there were tears in Clara's eyes. But he had to remember those tears were Maria's not Clara's.

It didn't matter though. He wanted to jump up on that stage and wrap her in his arms.

When the curtain closed and reopened he found that he'd been the first to his feet with his applause. Or he thought he was. Carlos Keller was a swift man.

As Clara took her curtain call, center stage, she looked down at him and blew him a kiss.

He already knew he'd fallen in love with her, which he also knew was a big mistake. But the crushing tightness in his chest at that moment nearly had him on his knees. It was mutual love and a mutual respect for each other that made fate intertwine their lives at that stop light.

His mother didn't love him—nor had his grandmother or Patricia Little for that matter. That woman on stage, who had been kissing that other guy, she loved him. She respected him, and she'd sleep in his arms tonight and wake in them tomorrow.

Warner's applause grew louder until his hands had gone numb.

When the curtain closed, he turned to see Madeline smiling up at him. It wasn't just a happy smile as though she'd watched her daughter give an amazing performance. This was a happy mother smile—happy that he was there, happy that he loved her daughter.

A lump formed in his throat. He turned to follow Ed out of the aisle. And as every Keller cleared the aisle they turned back and gave him some kind of reassuring look or gesture that said Clara's success was his success. It was a gesture a family would make.

The lump in his throat grew and landed in his stomach as a large boulder.

They were accepting him into their family. For the first time in his life he was part of something more than just him. He was part of a family and the feeling was nearly as overwhelming as the love he'd found he had for Clara.

Ed was right—you don't mess with the Keller family.

Patricia Little was going down.

CHAPTER 23

*C*lara ran her finger tips over Warner's chest as she lay in bed with him. This wasn't what she thought she'd be doing with her life—shacking up with a man she didn't really know. But it felt so right.

"Ed said you confronted some guy tonight at the theater."

She felt his breath hitch before he eased back against the pillow again. "Reviewer. Or someone Patty paid to take some pictures and give you a bad review."

"I've had bad reviews before."

"Sure, buried in the back of a newspaper. I will guarantee she will have this to discuss on that stupid show next week."

"Good thing there are only three more shows, huh?"

He chuckled and kissed the top of her head. "You're something."

"I hope you'll always think so." She rolled so that she lay atop him and looked down into his eyes. "Why do you want to sell your songs? Why don't you record them and sell you?"

Warner reached up and tucked her hair behind her ear. "I've had too many people tell me I wouldn't sell."

"I don't think they're right."

"I seem to have you hypnotized."

Clara leaned down and kissed him softly. "I think I have my wits about me, and I'm free all next week."

"Oh, yeah." He laughed. "I am too. The joys of unemployment."

"From Monday morning until Friday night we are going to record and write."

Warner pushed his head further into the pillow to look up at her. "Clara, I can't take you away from what you're already doing so that I can chase some silly dream."

"If I thought it was silly I would have told you so. But something tells me there will be a day when the tour bus belongs to you and Patricia Little is serving me my Starbucks."

Warner pulled her to him and rolled her until she was on her back and he was pressed against her.

"I've never said this to another person in my life," he sucked in a breath. "I love you."

Her eyes misted as she looked up at him. "You do?"

He nodded. "I've never felt like this before in my life. This is crazy, right?"

Clara wrapped her arms around his neck. "Not in my world."

"I'm glad I happened into your world."

"So am I," she said as she pulled him closer and kissed him again.

He was never going to sleep anywhere else again. She was keeping Warner Wright for the rest of her life.

WARNER HAD BEEN RIGHT. THE NEXT MORNING THERE WAS A horrid review in the paper about Clara's performance. She had read it no less than a dozen times before Darcy snatched the paper out of her hands.

Darcy sat down at the table in Arianna's office and looked at her. "You're not going down with this."

"I know. It still stings."

"It's made up."

Clara nodded. "I don't understand hurting someone just for publicity. Warner has never done anything to that woman."

"Sure he has. He's made her very famous."

Clara snorted a laugh. "How has he done that?"

Darcy threw the paper toward her. "By failing miserably."

That stung as bad as the review. "He's not a failure."

"He is when she keeps setting him up to do so." Darcy leaned in on her arms. "Look, she's not famous because she's nice. She's riding this fame and fortune all the way on being nasty. People eat that up." She sat back in her chair. "Admit it. She was why you watched that stupid show. You wanted to see a cat fight."

Clara had to smile at that. She was right. She'd watched it faithfully just to see who got in the woman's way. She just never would have guessed that she'd fall in love with the step-son Patricia Little detested or that she'd be one of those people that Patricia stepped on.

Darcy pulled her phone out of her purse and began to scroll through items on the screen. "So, I have six reviewers coming from different papers. I have two news stations coming to do a piece on the theater and you. One at the matinee and one at the evening's performance."

"You did that?"

"You betcha, sister." She scrolled through a few more items. "And Summer should be here in an hour to go through a quick run through with Duke for Sunday's final performance."

Clara felt her mouth fall open. "Excuse me? The paper says I was that bad, but I wasn't."

Darcy grinned as she slid her phone back into her purse. "You have a performance that night with your lover man."

"I told him I couldn't do it. Randy was going to back him up."

"Yeah, well Randy knows who is coming to listen to you two

perform. You'd better find a few minutes between playing Maria and lying in bed to practice."

"Darcy!"

Her sister-in-law cackled a laugh. "Prove that Little woman wrong. Make the world hear Warner Wright. Together you can do this."

"You really think so?"

"You love him don't you?"

Clara's shoulders dropped. "I do. I really do."

"Then it'll all work out." She reached her hand across the table and covered Clara's. "Trust me. I know what I'm talking about."

Darcy did know what she was talking about. Love could win out over everything if they just worked as a team.

A warmth moved through her. She would get to be there when Warner performed. She thought he should perform his new song, the one he wrote on the back of his eviction notice. The thought made her laugh. He was such a musician. They often got so into what they were doing they never noticed the obvious —such as the notice.

Well, whatever Patricia Little's purpose was in kicking him out of his home it had worked in Clara's favor. Warner was more of a Keller than he knew. He belonged with them.

She looked down at her wrist at the infinity tattoo and the word family which was written into the design. Darcy had a matching one as well. The thought made her smile, maybe Warner needed some ink.

CHAPTER 24

*J*ust as the curtain rose on the first act of the matinee, Carrie, the ticket counter girl, tapped Clara on the shoulder.

"He's here. He even bought a ticket and one for tonight."

Clara turned to her. "You let him buy tickets?"

Carrie smiled. "He was very final about it."

Clara smiled and gave Carrie a nod. Clara had told Carrie to watch for Warner, though she hadn't expected him to come. Warner should have been writing songs and practicing, but he had even bought a ticket to see her perform.

Suddenly she was more nervous that she'd ever remembered being. At least at last night's show she knew where he would be. She knew where to look and where not to look. Tonight he hid, among the many reviewers, in the seats of the small but crowded theater.

It shouldn't be like any other night, so she wasn't going to let it be.

Soon it was time for her to make her way into Tony's life and forget about Warner. But in a mere few hours it looked as though she'd be changing careers. She was about to be performer of a whole new kind. She was the voice to Warner's songs, unless she could convince him that he should be, then she'd be along for the amazing ride.

WARNER WAS POSSIBLY IN THE FURTHEST SEAT FROM THE STAGE, but he liked it. This way he could really focus on her and the crowd.

It was hard to focus at all; he had to admit to himself. He had a song running though his head and he needed to get it on paper.

He could have stayed home and worked all day. Clara hadn't asked him to come see her, but he'd wanted to. He'd found the review from the man he'd confronted the night before. It was nasty, just as Patricia had promised it would be. But when Clara hit the stage anyone in that audience who had seen the review knew it was all lies.

She was remarkable—though he knew she would be. And next week she'd promised they'd record all week. By the end of the week he'd have his demos. But even that thought wasn't right anymore. He wanted more.

Oh, having a woman love him and believe in him gave him a whole new lease on life. No longer did he want anyone else to sing his songs. He wanted to sing them. And why not? He was the one who felt them. It would be nice if she'd sing them with him.

After hearing what she and Randy had done to Love Song, he simply couldn't imagine anyone else recording it.

Then he thought about Jordan Farr sitting on Patricia's couch. He'd thought perhaps the man would have given him a chance. He'd been the only one not to shut the door in Warner's face. It was no use. He was just going to have to battle Patricia till the bitter end. Only now he wanted to. He had a secret weapon, and her name was Clara Keller.

At intermission the lights came up and Warner stood to

stretch his legs. The man next to him turned toward him. "Are you Warner Wright?"

His chest tightened and he felt as though he'd been socked in the stomach. "Yes."

"I thought so." The man eagerly extended his hand toward him. "Jeremy Smith, with Smith-Parks Entertainment."

The tightening in his chest continued as he shook the man's hand. Smith-Parks Entertainment was the company that had first put the Nashville Ex's on TV, before selling it off to a bigger studio. Warner could feel his jaw tighten.

"I hear you're a song writer," Jeremy Smith said with an enthusiastic smile.

"I am."

"And I hear that Clara Keller is going to be recording your songs."

This man was good. He had some spies in some pretty remote places. "Yes, that's the plan. She'll be the voice on the demo tracks."

"I'd love to talk to you about a new show I'm putting together. It'll follow the careers of three different song writers and singers trying to make it to the top. You have a great angle already."

And there was the catch. The man knew that if he could get Warner on TV and Patricia could get her claws into him even more publicly it would be a TV frenzy.

"Mr. Smith, I appreciate it. But I certainly don't have the same appeal that Patricia Little does. I don't think anyone would want to watch me."

Jeremy Smith's smile didn't diminish. He pulled a card out of his shirt pocket and handed it to Warner. "I hate Patricia Little. If I'd have cast her, I'd have kicked her off the show. They hired her after I sold the rights."

Warner looked at the business card and then back at the man standing before him.

Jeremy reached for his coat which hung over the back of his

seat. "Give it some thought. I'll be in touch. You have a good nature, Warner. I think people would be happy to see it, especially now that they know what kind of bitch you grew up with."

Jeremy started out of the aisle and turned back. "By the way, I was here last night too. Her performance was spot on and that review that weasel put up about her was phony. I brought a few tonight to write some real reviews." He gave Warner a wave. "We'll talk soon."

Warner looked back down at the card. It was as if he were holding Willy Wonka's Golden Ticket. He could have everything he'd ever wanted if he just didn't mess it up.

CHAPTER 25

*J*eremy Smith hadn't come back to the vacant seat. Not that Warner had really expected him to.

Now Warner's head was buzzing with the thought of the TV show. That song was still whirling around in his head and Clara was kissing that guy on stage again.

He looked down at the card to take his mind off of that kiss.

When the show was over, Warner poured out of the theater with the rest of the patrons and waited in the lobby. Clara probably didn't even know he was there. Would she know to come find him?

He took out his cell phone, turned it on, and the text message pinged in his hand.

I'll find you when I've changed. Thank you for coming.

So the girl at the ticket counter did tell her he was there.

Warner looked up from his phone and a man stood right before him. "Warner Wright? Can I interview you?"

He felt as though he were walking in some alternate universe.

"And you are. . ."

"Sorry. Cal Carson. I'm with channel five."

"Right. What can I do for you?"

"I just wanted to get your take on the performance and the theater."

Warner looked at the man, who now held his iPhone out in front of him as a recording device just to catch his voice, but he didn't have a camera.

"I thought the performance was spectacular."

Cal raised an eyebrow. "Anything else?"

"What else can I say? The theater puts on top notch entertainment and has since they opened." He knew because Madeline had made sure to tell him how amazing Clara was as Annie. "The music is superb, the sets are fantastic, and of course the actors were amazing."

Cal nodded. "Clara Keller. How do you think her performance rated over last night's performance?"

Ah, there we go he thought. "Both nights were perfectly executed. Her timing, her voice, her emotional delivery. I can say I've never seen Maria done better."

Cal hit the button on his phone and held out his hand to Warner. "Thank you for your time."

Warner narrowed his eyes on him. "Is that all you wanted to ask me?"

"Most certainly was."

He nodded. "Mr. Carson, it was a pleasure."

Cal Carson walked away as Clara emerged from the door behind him.

"Was that Cal Carson from TV you were just talking to?"

He turned and kissed her cheek. "Yes it was."

"What did he want?"

"He wanted to know what I thought about the performance."

She bit her lip. "He wanted to know why last night sucked and this one didn't? Did he want to know why Patricia Little hates me now too?"

Warner ran his tongue over his teeth. "No. I was a little

surprised her name didn't come up at all. I certainly thought it would have."

"So he only asked you about your thoughts on the show."

"Yup."

She grinned that sexy grin he'd been getting used to. "And you told him you thought I was absolutely amazing?"

"I did."

"Really, Warner, that's all that matters." She rose up on her toes and gave him a gentle kiss. "Okay, I'm starving and I only have an hour to eat."

"Doesn't give us much time."

"Deli around the corner. C'mon."

WITHIN THE HOUR THEY WERE BACK AT THE THEATER, CLARA WAS in her dressing room, and he was standing at the bar, sipping on a soda.

"Sticking around for the next show?" Arianna asked as she moved up next to him.

"Of course."

She smiled easily. "I wasn't sure that girl was ever going to fall in love. Looks like the right guy just hadn't driven by her yet."

He swallowed hard. "She's had a lot of relationships?"

Arianna shook her head and the woman behind the bar handed her a bottle of water. Arianna smiled at her, opened it and took a sip. "No. Clara was always one who was into enjoying her life with no strings attached. She liked her work here. She loves her friends. Her goals were more important."

' That stung Warner in the chest. None of that sounded like the Clara he knew. She was willing to give up everything to sing his songs and get them recorded. His mouth went dry and his took another sip of his soda.

"I've seen how she looks at you," Arianna continued. "I've been lucky enough to be part of a family that waits for that perfect person. And when that perfect person comes along we scoop them up."

"And you think she thinks that about me?"

"I do."

He felt the heat rise under his collar. "I don't know that I'm too good for anyone. I've never had much of a family."

"Then it looks like you fell into the right one." She rested her hand on his. "You fit in with the Kellers just fine."

She turned and walked toward her office leaving him sitting there. His head spun and his stomach did a funny little flip.

It had only been two weeks and he'd already moved in and told Clara he loved her. Seriously, things never moved like that did they? But in this family they seemed to. In this family that was expected and accepted.

Maybe he'd better think about it really hard.

Was this what he wanted? Not the career or the music, but the woman—the family?

He had to unbutton the top button on his shirt so he could breathe. It was what he wanted and he never knew it was in him to want that. He wanted to marry Clara Keller and make her his. And he wouldn't suffocate her and make her hate him like his father must have done with Warner's mother and Patty. He would take care of her and love her. If she still wanted to kiss men on stage, he'd let her, even if he didn't like it. If he did get that tour bus he'd want her right there with him.

He looked down at his hands. They shook. This was certainly not what he thought he'd be thinking about when he'd awakened this morning. But now he knew what he needed—wanted to do. He had to ask Clara Keller to be his wife.

CHAPTER 26

*C*lara had slept in on Sunday morning and she felt refreshed. The warmth of the sun touched her skin and the sounds of a Sunday morning kept her calm. But she realized she didn't hear the soft breathing of the man she loved as she turned to see his side of the bed empty.

She touched his pillow, it was cold. He'd been out of bed for a while. Clara looked at the clock on the night stand, it was ten o'clock.

Well, she couldn't blame him for getting up and going about his day. She stretched and then rolled out of bed and headed to the shower.

When she was dressed, and her hair pulled back in a ponytail, she headed downstairs to find Warner. The house was just as quiet downstairs as well. She thought he might be recording or playing in the basement, but the lights were off and no sound came up the stairs. It was then she looked outside and his truck was gone.

It was normal to wonder where he went. There were no notes lying around. She looked at her cell phone on the counter—no text message either. She typed a text on her phone to Warner and hit send. A few moments later his phone buzzed in the front room.

There his phone sat on the table.

Clara blew out a breath. She needed to not get worked up over him not being there. She didn't have any ownership on him. He was a free man to do what he wanted to do, but a note would have been nice. And damnit, who leaves their phone on the table?

The thought made her settle and laugh. Warner, that's who.

Wasn't that what she loved about the man? He was unpredictable and a little off center? He was probably afraid to wake her up and he was down the street writing some song with the dog behind that bent down chain link fence.

He'd come home when he was ready. And as long as that time was before the time they needed to perform, everything would be fine.

BUT BY THREE O'CLOCK IN THE AFTERNOON, CLARA HAD GROWN worried.

There was no one she could call and she had no idea where he might have gone. It was evident she didn't know this man at all.

She'd cleaned and scrubbed the entire house. She'd called Darcy and acted as if she were just calling to chat, but she was sure Darcy saw right through that.

Then she heard the sound of his old truck pulling up in front of the house. It was about damn time. Who did he think he was?

She started for the door, her hand on the knob, and fire burning through her.

Clara swung open the door in a fury only to see a completely uncoordinated Warner trying to carry bags of groceries, what looked like bags of clothes, and a vase with a dozen roses up the front steps.

It was as if water had flooded her veins and the fire in her was gone. She hurried to him.

"Let me help you."

"Take the roses. Take the roses," he said as he nearly threw them at her as his fingers gave way.

"Where have you been all day?"

"Shopping. I hate shopping." He walked up the steps and into the house dropping the bags on the couch.

Clara closed the front door. "Why all the shopping?"

"I thought I'd better have something nice to wear tonight. I only have two pairs of jeans and about four ratty shirts."

She knew that, she'd done his laundry and she'd tossed out a few things. She looked him over. "You got a haircut too."

He ran his hand over his hair. "Does it look okay? I think it's too short."

Clara set the vase of roses on the coffee table and turned to Warner. She ran her fingers through his newer, more hip, do. "I like it."

He let out a breath. "Well, really that's all that matters."

His shoulders had finally dropped and he seemed more relaxed as he slid his hands to her waist. "I'm sorry I didn't call. I can't find my phone."

"It's right here on the table." Clara nodded to the coffee table where he'd buried the phone with the bags.

"Oh. I should memorize your number. I didn't know how to get a hold of you. And I should always be able to get hold of you." His voice softened as he spoke.

"I'll write it down and put it in the glove compartment of your truck."

He smiled as he pressed his forehead to hers. "I like how you think."

"We make a good team."

Clara felt him tense as she rested her hands on his chest. He shifted his eyes to hers. "You really think so?"

"I do think so. And tonight we're going to show them all what a great team we make."

Warner moved his head back and now looked directly at her. "Tonight we're going to show them?"

She smiled and rose up on her toes, wrapping her arms around his neck. "Darcy set it up so that my understudy closes out the run and I'll be there to perform with my man."

She saw his Adam's apple bob as he swallowed hard. "Wow. They did that for me?"

"For us." She set herself back on the ground and gave him a hard stare. "I'm in on this Warner. You and me. We're going to sell more than your songs. We're going to sell you. You deserve the glory and stardom that come with the lyrics. You're an amazing song writer and you're being sold short because of one bitch who won't shut up when she should."

His eyes lightened and a smile formed on his lips. "Wow, I really do love you."

"Don't tease me now. Because now I'm getting pissy."

"No. No teasing. It's just amazing that you'll do this for me."

"I told you I love you. I don't just use those words haphazardly."

He nodded. "I know. I've met your family. You all mean it when you say it and you hold on tight when you find the right person."

She narrowed her eyes on him. "Who were you talking to?"

"Most recently your aunt. But what you have comes across loud and clear."

Clara nodded. "Why the roses?"

His eye brows knitted and then rose as he tried to keep up with her shift in conversation. "They're for you for closing night."

Clara smiled. "You're very thoughtful."

"Well, they have a dual purpose. And now that you're going to be performing with me this changes things."

CHAPTER 27

*W*arner stepped away from her and ran his hand over his hair as if he'd forgotten that his longer locks were gone. He turned back to her.

"I've had a lot of things going on since last night. I got an offer to do a reality TV show."

Clara bit down on the inside of her cheek as she thought about that. Why hadn't he said anything? Then she remembered she'd had him undressed and in bed before he could have. But that was really a big offer.

"What kind of show?"

"They'll follow song writers and musicians trying to make it."

"It would give you exposure."

"It'll give Patty something to shoot down."

"And the world will actually see she's wrong."

He nodded. "Something else came to mind last night too and I wasn't ready for it."

Clara watched him collect his thoughts. Suddenly she was afraid she didn't fit into this new plan of his.

He paced the floor and then looked up at her. "I'm not a

family man. Not that I don't want to be. I just don't know how to be."

"Okay," she drawled out, confused as to what he was trying to tell her.

"Your family has really embraced me the past few weeks—all of them."

"That's what Kellers do." She put her hands on her hips. "Warner, what are you trying to say?"

He scratched the back of his head. "I never thought I'd be the kind of man to get married or settle down. I'd never thought about having kids or owning a house."

Clara could feel the sting of tears starting in her eyes. He was going to dump her. It was coming and she was going to blow when he finally delivered the last words of this little speech he was working up to.

"Spill it, Warner." Her voice was edgy. "Just get it over with, would you? I have things to do."

He nodded with his eyes wide. He stepped toward her and took her hands in his. She noticed immediately that his hands shook. "The roses are because I don't have anything else to offer you."

Clara swallowed hard. Here it comes, she thought.

"I didn't know I'd be doing this when I saw you at that stop light. But, Clara, will you marry me? And I mean, will you marry me soon? Let's elope next week. Do the shows with me. Be my partner. I don't have anything to support you. I don't even have a ring. That's what the flowers are for. I can't..."

She'd lost track of all the other things he was babbling about. "Whoa!" She sucked in a breath. "Warner, I was ready for you to tell me you were leaving."

He took a step back. "Why would I leave?"

"You're out of sorts."

He laughed. "All the damn time. But I love you."

Clara's head was spinning and then she let out a chuckle.

"Let's back up. You bought me the roses so you could ask me to marry you?"

Warner nodded quickly. "Yeah. I realized that was what I wanted more than anything when I was talking to your aunt last night."

Clara understood it now. "And you want to elope?"

He nodded again. "I don't want to wait. And your aunt made it clear that the Kellers, when they find the right person they snatch them up. Well, maybe the Wrights should do that too. I mean if only my family would have gone after what they wanted maybe my life would have been a little different."

She wrapped her arms around his neck again. "Warner, you did go after everything you wanted. Look at all you've done on your own. The jobs, the college degrees, the music. I do think you're a Keller at heart."

"That's a pretty big statement."

"And it's true."

Warner wrapped his arms around her waist and pulled her to him. "Okay, but you haven't answered me."

Clara's stomach was filled with butterflies as she looked into Warner's eyes. She'd never been nervous, but he gave her this new buzz. "I'll be your partner. Whatever it takes to get you sold. Do the show, Warner. Let them show the world who you are." She sucked in a breath. "Now, I'll let you know what I think about eloping, that's going to take some thought. But, I will tell you, I would love to be your wife."

His eyes opened wide. "Really? You'd want to marry me?"

"You asked me to didn't you?"

"Yeah, I did. I just didn't think you'd want to."

"Are you backing down?"

Warner shook his head. "No. No. I want this more than anything. I've just never had anyone want me back in return."

Clara pressed her lips to his. "I'm never letting you go. So you'd better decide this is what you want forever."

He let out a breath. "It's what I want."

"Good answer." She kissed him again. "I'll tell you what. Let's see how it goes tonight and then maybe we can plan a trip to Vegas next weekend."

"Really? You'll marry me that quick?"

Clara shrugged. "I've never been one for big flashy events like overdone weddings. But maybe next month or so we can have a big reception."

"I'd like that."

Clara rested her head against Warner's chest where she could feel his heart race against her cheek. "So would I."

CHAPTER 28

*T*here wasn't much time for celebrating their pending nuptials. They had a show to get ready for in a few hours and they needed to practice.

Warner was going to have to carry most of the show himself, but that was okay by Clara. This was his music, his opportunity, and his dream. She would be the woman behind the man. There always was one—the one who kept it all together, she amused herself with the thought.

When Warner was in work mode—he was in work mode. It was as if a little demon appeared when he talked. She'd seen the kind before. The music made them mad with a passion and it was nearly relayed in anger. There'd be no reason to get upset when he wanted to start a song over and over. She knew once the night was over he'd simmer and be back to normal.

Once they'd run through the short play list, which they only had twenty minutes to perform, they got dressed. Clara was more than impressed with Warner's choice of clothes he'd purchased.

"I very much like how your ass looks in those jeans," she said leaning up against the doorjamb.

"I hate shopping. Did I mention that?"

"You mentioned it."

He finally looked up at her. "Oh, Lord, you look good."

"You think so? Too casual?"

He shook his head. "No. Just right."

She gave him a wink and turned to walk back into the bathroom.

"Hey," he called from the other room. "Your ass looks good in your jeans too."

She only smiled and kept moving toward the vanity.

The curl in her hair probably wouldn't last under the lights, but she'd sprayed it stiff. Her eye makeup was heavy, but she liked the smoky look to them. The flowy cotton shirt was the same one she'd worn when she and Randy had performed at The Stage. She liked it best. Usually she'd wear her boots with the ensemble, but she was really wanting to wear a pair of heels tonight. She'd put the boots in the Jeep just in case she changed her mind.

Randy hadn't told her who was going to be there to listen to them. But she did wonder if Jeremy Smith had anything to do with the booking date.

She had told him to accept the TV show proposal, but she wondered how much that would just feed Patricia Little's need to tear Warner down.

Clara wasn't going to think about it. First she needed to get through the night. And then she needed to decide if she was going to tell her family that she was running away to get married, or if she should save that news for later.

SUNDAY NIGHT AND THE BAR WAS PACKED. WARNER HAD TO wonder if the people of Nashville had a life.

Randy was already there and ready to back him up, but he hadn't looked surprised when he saw Clara and gave her a big hug. Perhaps Warner had been the last one to know she'd be performing with him.

All the better, he decided. That way he hadn't had too much time to piss her off by practicing over and over before the show.

"You ready, Warner?" Randy placed his hand on his shoulder.

"I suppose."

"I heard you already met Jeremy Smith."

"I met him."

Randy flicked the guitar pick in his hand with his thumb. "You gonna do it? The show?"

"Clara thinks I should."

"Wouldn't hurt, that's for sure."

It would when Patricia Little got word of it.

Randy walked away and Clara moved in closer to him, her guitar already hanging in front of her.

"Ready?"

It would be a lie if he told her yes. "I will be."

"Jeremy Smith is here."

Warner looked out and saw him sitting at a table, there were others with him, their backs were turned to the stage. Knowing it was Jeremy Smith that was there to hear him put him at ease. He'd already met the guy and decided to work with him. Suddenly the set before him didn't seem as daunting.

Though, he had noticed the entire table of Kellers waving up at him. He gave them a short wave back and moved out of sight of the audience.

He'd better not slip up and say anything about running away with his now fiancée. He'd better not even call her his fiancée.

The performer on stage ahead of them finished his set and the emcee for the night took the mic. A strange calm took over Warner's body when he looked at Clara all gussied up and looking like a star. She was going to be his wife in a matter of days. That would be more wild than any performance he could ever give. The man in the audience wanted to have him on his TV show. That too was going to be quite an experience. Warner's nerves kicked up when he looked out and saw Carlos looking up at him with his dark, stern eyes. The night had been fine until then. But Madeline reached over and touched Carlos's shoulder, and he'd softened just as she'd spoken to him. That was what Warner wanted now, that kind of connection, and he had that with Clara.

"Okay, here we go," Clara turned to him and said.

"I love you."

"I love you too. Now let's knock 'em dead."

TWENTY MINUTES, THAT'S ALL THEY HAD TO SELL THEIR GOODS AND prove to this specific crowd that Warner Wright was worth showing off to the world. Randy had conveniently made himself nearly unnoticeable, but Clara shined like the star Warner thought she was.

They had killed it on Love Songs and his song Give It Up, which Clara had noted was his jaded song. When they started their finale with the song he'd written on the back of his eviction notice, the crowd was on their feet.

It was only then that he noticed the woman at the table with Jeremy Smith was the platinum recording artist Savannah. A talent so big and a star so bright she only needed one name, just like Madonna or Cher.

Clara must not have noticed because her voice was solid and her chords were strong.

When he saw Clara's father smiling and dancing with his wife, Warner knew they had a hit. The right person just had to hear it.

As they finished with the big finale he looked into Clara's eyes. The curls she'd worried about had fallen limp and her hair framed her face. Her dark eyes were seductive and burning right there in front of God and the world—and they were meant for him.

They were a team and damn it felt good.

When the music stopped and the crowd before them was still on their feet and hollering their names he pulled Clara to him, as close as they could get with their instruments between them, and planted a kiss on her lips.

Thank goodness she'd been driving down the street singing at the top of her lungs. He was glad he wasn't going to miss a moment with her.

CHAPTER 29

*T*hey moved back stage and the electricity between the three of them was incredible.

"Did you see her?" Randy had a hand on each of their shoulders. "Did you see who was with Jeremy Smith?"

"Savannah!" Carla shouted as she jumped up and down. "Oh, Warner, when she heard Kick em' Where it Counts did you see her eyes light up? To think you just threw that together the other day and she wants it. You could see it. She wants it!" She was jumping up and down and all Warner could do was smile.

"Did anyone notice she left the building?" Warner said calmly as the other two looked around the curtain.

"Doesn't mean anything." Clara shrugged. "Her people will call your people."

"I don't have people."

"You have Jeremy Smith and he's still out there waiting for you. So get your guitar stored and get out there and talk to the man."

Warner nodded. He held his hand out to Randy. "Thanks for supporting me."

"Hey, man, you have a great sound."

That meant a lot coming from a man who was on his way to something big. Warner couldn't wait to be that man too.

CLARA WENT IMMEDIATELY TO HER FAMILY. WARNER GAVE THEM A wave and walked over to Jeremy Smith. He knew Clara would fill them in and they'd forgive him for being rude and not saying hello.

When Jeremy saw him approach the table, he stood and held out his hand to him.

"Warner, that was great. You sounded amazing."

"Thank you, sir. I appreciate that."

"Please, have a seat. Can I offer you a drink? Jack and Coke?"

Warner smiled pleasantly. "Just a Coke would be fine."

Jeremy nodded and waved down a waitress to order drinks and then turned back to Warner.

"Have you given any thought to my proposal from yesterday? I have one space left and it's all yours."

Warner could feel his palms grow damp as his heart rate kicked up. "I have been thinking about it. And Clara and I were talking—and she thinks it would be a great opportunity for me to showcase my talents."

"She's very smart. That's exactly what we want to do. I've seen you. I know a few artists that are making it big that don't have as good a sound as you. And your writing style is fantastic."

"Thank you."

Jeremy leaned in over the table. "You did see who was here didn't you?"

"I thought I saw Savannah."

"You sure did. She's looking for talent to open for her on tour. She had good things to say."

That heat burned through his core again. His day was coming. He could feel it! Maybe when the ride was over he could teach again and no one would think twice of it.

He let out a breath. Where had that come from?

Well, no matter. This was the here and now. This was the life of a man who was going to elope with the woman of his dreams, be on a new TV show, and he was taking the comment as a sign that he'd be touring with Savannah. Now he just had to turn his body around and head to the Keller's table and look Carlos Keller in the eye.

Hard times were ahead.

WHEN JEREMY SMITH FINISHED HIS DRINK HE SHOOK WARNER'S hand again and said he'd be in touch in a few days. He strode out of the bar as if he owned the whole town and Warner turned and walked toward the Keller's table.

Darcy jumped out of her chair and ran toward him throwing her arms around his neck. He had no choice but to grab hold and let her hug him.

"Oh-my-God! You were amazing. Just amazing. And you wrote all those songs. Oh-my-God!"

He laughed as he set her back on her feet and she smiled up at him.

"Thank you. I'm glad you enjoyed the set," Warner said as Ed walked up and shook his hand.

"Enjoyed it? She was screaming like you were Dierks Bently or something."

"That's quite an honor to be compared."

Darcy smacked Ed on the arm. "You were wonderful. And we saw who was here. Isn't that exciting?"

"Very exciting." Warner tried to keep a calm in his voice.

It was then he noticed Carlos stand and move toward him, and Warner's mouth went dry.

Carlos held his hand out and shook Warner's. "That was a fine show you put on."

"Thank you, sir. I couldn't do it without Clara and Randy."

Carlos nodded. "Oh, I think you could." He placed his hand on Warner's shoulder turning him slightly. "How about we step outside and get some air?"

He started for the door and Warner was sure he could feel his knees grow weaker. He turned to look at Clara, but she was deep in conversation with her mother.

Carlos was outside and already leaned up against the building when Warner made it through the crowd by the bar.

"Starting to get colder," Carlos said looking up at the sky.

"Sure is."

Carlos had his feet crossed at his ankles and his thumbs tucked into the front pockets of his jeans.

Warner stood there in the awkward silence and prayed for mercy.

"This kinda takes Clara out of her normal line of performing."

"Yes, sir, it does. She was doing me a great favor by being here tonight."

He nodded. "Must have meant a great deal to her to give up her last night on stage."

"I never asked her to do that, sir. She said it was planned and she'd be here. I'd never ask her to give up anything for me."

Carlos stood up straight, his thumbs still tucked into his pockets. "She's a smart woman."

"Yes, sir, she is."

"She wouldn't fall into the wrong crowd or follow something she didn't have a passion for."

"I agree."

"She seems to have fallen for you and that scares me to death."

The pain in Warner's chest felt as if Carlos had shoved a knife into his heart.

"Sir, I don't mean her…"

Carlos held his hand up. "I'm her father. It's supposed to scare me to death." He rested his hand on Warner's shoulder. "Clara is thirty years old. She's old enough to make her own decisions."

Warner had no more words. He only nodded.

"I want her happy and taken care of."

"Sir, I have every intention of taking care of her and making her happy forever."

Carlos dropped his hand. "Forever, huh?"

"Yes, sir. I have no intention of just being someone in passing. I would like to spend the rest of my life with Clara."

Carlos bit down on his lip and looked out to the street. "You're saying you plan on a lifetime?" he asked and then looked back at Warner.

"Yes, sir. I do. And if I may, I know it's only been a few weeks, but I'd love to have your blessing on that lifetime."

Carlos rubbed the back of his neck. "It sounds like you've given this some thought."

"I have."

"I thought you moving in was a little fast. This seems even faster."

"I wouldn't have moved in had I thought it was short term."

"That Little woman on TV doesn't have anything nice to say about you."

Of all the times for Patty's opinions of him to affect his life, this wasn't the time.

"Those are her own opinions, sir. I don't have anything to do with her."

Carlos smiled. "I know. You handle her criticisms very well."

"Again, those are her own opinions. I continue to do what I can to build my career."

"Warner, I think you're going to do just great, career wise. And if Clara sees something in you then I know Ms. Little is wrong about you."

"Thank you. That means a lot."

"As for that lifetime thing," Carlos blew out a breath. "It scares me to death."

"Me too."

Carlos laughed. "It should. Women are strange creatures, but worth it."

"I think so too."

"If Clara chooses you then you have my blessing."

Warner's limbs went numb. "Thank you. Thank you very much."

He wanted to hug him, but at this point Warner would probably start to cry.

Carlos nodded. "Do you fish?"

"I haven't fished since I was a young boy in Memphis."

"Curtis and I are planning a trip in a few weeks before it gets too cold. I think we convinced Ed to come along. Why don't you join us?"

"I'd like that."

Carlos placed his hand back on Warner's shoulder as they turned back for the bar. "We can have this discussion again when there is a stream of moving water to throw you in," he said with a laugh, but Warner wondered if secretly Carlos already knew their plan.

CHAPTER 30

*C*lara opened the back door to the house and turned on the kitchen lights as Warner cleared the last step.

"I'm not home for three days and you move a man in the house?" Christian's voice rang out from the living room.

"Hey, my name is on the lease now, not yours."

Christian limped into the kitchen, a bag of peas wrapped to his knee with an ace bandage. "Just saying it would have been nice to have been told."

Warner walked through the door and shut it behind him. "Sorry. Did I interrupt?"

"No, man. I'm just busting her chops. How was your show?"

"It was good," Warner said walking up to Clara, wrapping his arm around her waist. "Your sister was phenomenal."

She slapped him on the arm and moved to the refrigerator, pulling out two bottles of water. "It wasn't about me. It was about this very talented man. Did you know they want to put him on a TV show? That's right. He's going to be a huge star."

Warner took the bottle of water she offered him and opened it quickly. He had a hard time hearing people brag about him. It certainly wasn't something he was used to.

"TV?" Christian considered. "That's cool. Sell any of your songs yet?"

Warner swallowed the water he'd just taken in. "I'm hoping the TV show will help me do that. Though, I think if I could get someone to sign me, I'd really like to do more than sell my music."

"Seems to me there'd be a lot more money in it."

"I'm not in it for the money. I love music," he said and by the look on Christian's face he knew he understood doing something for the love of it.

"Did you know Warner has a degree in music? He's a music teacher," Clara added.

"Was."

"Was, until Patricia Little got involved. But the point is, Jeremy Smith wants you on TV and Savannah was there checking you out."

Christian took a step closer to them. "Savannah? Savannah was there?"

Clara's eyes widened. "She was. Oh, Chris, you should have seen her. She was dressed casual, but she has that hair, you know that massive hair! She's so beautiful. But she was there with Jeremy Smith. She was there to see my Warner."

"That's cool, man."

Warner shook his head. "I don't know anything about her being there, but she's looking for talent to open her shows. We'll see."

"You're so modest," Clara looked at him. "Celebrate just a little. Tonight was a huge success."

He supposed it was. He just didn't like to get his hopes up. That was part of his plan in eloping. The sooner the better and for once he'd have something in his life cemented into place.

· · ·

WARNER WATCHED CLARA SLEEP PEACEFULLY IN HIS ARMS AS THE breeze outside cast shadows on the wall in the moonlight. He was wise enough to absorb it all. Every moment was one to be cherished and he'd never forget this moment, or the moment her father gave him his blessing.

He understood that Carlos didn't really know he was doing that, but it made Warner feel better.

"Clara," he whispered as he brushed her hair from her face. "Are you awake?"

She stirred in his arms and slightly opened one eye. "Warner, what's wrong?"

"Nothing." He smiled.

"What time is it?"

"Three."

She shifted and opened both eyes slightly. "Why are you staring at me?"

"Because you're beautiful."

She let out a groan and tried to turn away, but he caught her chin with his finger and turned her back toward him.

"There is a flight for Vegas at ten. As of eleven last night there was still room on it."

Her eyes opened further. "What are you talking about?"

"Let's go to Vegas and we can be married by tonight. I don't want to wait."

He was comforted with the fact that she was smiling, but he could see it in her eyes. Clara still thought he was crazy.

She inched her body up on to her elbow and looked him in the eye. "Are you sure you want to do this?"

"Have you changed your mind?"

Her eyes softened. "No. I'll never change my mind on you. I love you."

Warner brushed her cheek with his thumb. "I love you too. I don't want to wait the rest the week. Besides your father had a little talk with me and as much as he could, he gives his approval of me."

Clara smiled widely. "I know he does. That means a lot."

"So let's go. I want to get married."

In the dark her smile flashed white. "How can I possibly turn that down?"

∽

Clara didn't like not being up front with her family, but there was an excitement that buzzed through her like no other as she boarded the plane for Las Vegas.

They hadn't gone back to sleep after Warner had awakened her with his thoughts on leaving right away. Luckily they had left the house before Christian had awakened. But, in true Keller tradition, because it was killing her more than anything, she left a note on the kitchen table.

Warner and I have left on a spontaneous vacation. We will be back on Thursday.

As the plane took off Clara rested her head on Warner's shoulder. "I think this is the craziest, most exciting thing I've ever done."

"Me too."

"I'm scared to death." She chuckled and Warner moved to look at her.

"Why?"

Clara sat up in her seat and interlaced her fingers with his. "This is forever. This isn't just some fun vacation we're taking. In a few hours I'll be your wife, and I just want to be the best wife any man could have."

Warner smiled. "I can't imagine you wouldn't be."

"Look, I've been around happily married people my whole life. Even when my parents were divorced they were nice to each other. My grandparents are in their nineties and they still hold hands and kiss. I'm worried that I'll be too much work at some point and you won't want to deal with that."

"I seriously thought I'd be the one having second thoughts not you."

"Oh, I'm not having second thoughts. I just want to be more to you than your mother was or than Patricia Little was. You deserve so much, Warner. I want to be the woman to give that to you."

Warner touched her cheek. "You already are. Just the other day I was thinking about how wonderful it'll be to have someone —always. You're right. I've never had that. I suppose I should be the one warning you that maybe I'm high maintenance. Maybe I'll be the one who feels like you're in my way." He let out a breath. "But know you're not in my way."

"I already know how you work." She rested her head on his shoulder again. "I've seen you disappear when you have a song buzzing in your head. I've seen you go tyrant when you want something right. I think this TV show is going to bring out a beast in you no one has ever seen, and I'm ready for that."

She felt him quake as if he were holding back tears. She gave him the moment to collect his dignity and didn't look at him.

"I'm glad I chased you down," he said placing a kiss on the top of her head.

"So am I. Now I'm going to take a nap since someone woke me up very early."

CHAPTER 31

*C*lara was more than surprised that there was a car waiting for them at the airport when they arrived.

"When did you schedule this?" she asked as the driver opened their door and then put their luggage in the trunk.

"I did it all this morning. It's amazing what you can do in this city when you have a internet."

The driver shut the door and Clara snuggled in close to Warner. "Have you ever been here?"

"Yeah. A couple times. Back when I was just a kid in the way. I think this trip will be happier."

Clara sat up and looked at him. "What do you mean kid in the way?"

"I told you my grandmother didn't much care for me."

"Right. She'd drag you out here?"

"Oh she dragged me out here and left me with some random aunt in a trailer park for a year."

Clara covered her mouth with her hand and she felt the tears stinging. "That's horrible. How can someone do that to a child?"

"Listen. It made me stronger. Don't go thinking I'll treat our children like that. A child should be the top priority if you choose to have them. Not just something you pass around."

Clara smiled. "I agree."

"In fact, the other day the thought of teaching crossed my mind again."

"I think you'd be a fantastic teacher."

He shrugged. "We'll see. I guess it hinges on Jeremy Smith now."

"And Savannah."

"I've been around the business long enough to know that you don't get too excited."

Clara shook her head. "Get a little excited. You're about to be hitched. Nothing is more exciting than that."

"Oh, I've done a few things to make it more exciting." Warner gave her a wink and she watched as the Las Vegas strip appeared before her.

The car drove them to the Bellagio and Clara couldn't help but bounce on the seat. "God, look at this place."

"Wait till you get inside."

"This is going to be wonderful."

"I hope you think so."

The driver took their bags and left them with the bellhop while Warner checked them in. Clara stood under the ceiling of glass flowers and let herself soak in the atmosphere.

"Are you ready, my sweet?" Warner offered her his arm.

"I sure am."

He led her to their room, which again was a surprise. It was a suite which faced the strip and a grand view of the fountains.

"Warner, this is beautiful."

"Not as beautiful as my view right now." He smiled at her as he shut the door.

Clara moved to him and wrapped her arms around his neck. "We're really going to do this aren't we?"

"I sure want to."

"So do I." She kissed him softly.

"Well, get settled in. You have an appointment to pick out a dress in an hour."

"A dress? Isn't that funny? I hadn't even thought about a dress."

He laughed. "I want you to have some elegance too. After all you're going to be stuck with this the rest of your life." He looked down at his worn jeans.

"I happen to like the view very much."

"I promise you'll have a better one for your wedding pictures."

He set the key card on the desk. "You will find the dress of your dreams. We get married at seven o'clock and have some magnificent pictures taken out front with the fountains."

"Thank you."

He pulled her to him. "No, thank you. I know going home and explaining this to everyone isn't going to be easy. I'm very much taking you out of your comfort zone here."

"You can't be comfortable always. Then you just get complacent." She winked and walked to the bedroom.

WARNER THOUGHT ABOUT WHAT SHE'D SAID. THAT WAS WHERE HE'D been for years—complacent in what he did. Meeting Clara had certainly changed that. He wanted to sing his own songs. He wanted to perform, get married, have a house full of kids, and damn—he wanted to teach again.

With Clara by his side there would be room for all of that. He let out a slow and steady breath.

"Time to grow up and be a man, Warner," he said to himself as he heard Clara squeal at the size of the tub.

He smiled. This was going to be the best vacation he'd ever planned.

CHAPTER 32

*C*lara had picked out a dress and Warner had surprised her again when he had a salon appointment for her as well. Her hair was done, makeup, fingers and toes. She found that he'd even arranged for a couples massage the next day.

No amount of planning for this special day could have made it any better.

Clara walked through the casino to the bank of elevators that would take her to her room when her phone rang.

She looked down at the screen. No surprise, Christian was hunting her down.

"Where are you?"

She pushed the button to the elevator. "I'm on vacation. I'll be home in a few days."

"Everyone is worried about you."

Clara sighed. "I'm thirty years old. I know what I'm doing."

"I do too."

She felt her heart rate accelerate. "What does that mean?"

"You're moving too fast. That's what that means. C'mon, you've only known Warner for a few weeks."

"What exactly is your point?"

"I told you my point. I think you're moving much too fast into this relationship."

Clara entered the elevator and quickly pushed the button for her floor hoping to ride alone.

"Christian, this is my life and my business. Ed and Darcy didn't know each other very long. Look at Curtis and Simone. I don't need you butting in here."

"I know where you are."

Clara bit down on her lip. "How do you know that?"

"I heard the sounds behind you."

She didn't know what to say.

Christian sighed into the phone. "Clara, who just leaves in the middle of the night and heads to Vegas?"

One thing about a close knit family, they knew everything without having the information first hand.

"I left you a note. I'm vacationing."

"Sure you are."

Now her nervousness churned in her stomach to anger. "This is none of your business."

"Don't you think mom and dad should be in on this?"

"No. No I don't. This is between me and Warner."

"So what are you doing on your vacation?"

The elevator slowed, the doors opened to the floor and Clara stepped out.

"Taking in the sights." There was a bite to her words.

"Clara," Christian's voice had softened enough to make her want to cry. But she wasn't going to cry. Her makeup was too nice.

"Chris, trust me. You have to know I would never do anything to harm myself or my family."

"I know."

"I love him. I love him very much."

"I don't doubt it." He let out a breath just as she arrived at her room. "Are you happy?"

"Happier than I've ever been."

"That's all that matters. I love you."

"I know you do, even if you're an ass."

He laughed. "I never promised I wouldn't be an ass as a big brother."

"I'll see you on Thursday."

"I'll be here." There was a moment of awkward silence as she slid her key card into the door. "Hey, give Warner my best."

The line went dead as she pushed open the door to the room.

The lights in the room were low as the sun was beginning to set. There was a bucket on the table with a bottle of champagne and two glasses. Warner must have had the room filled with six dozen roses.

He stepped out of the bedroom in a suit. His hair was groomed, his shadowed chin was bare. Those tears were back and she wasn't sure she could hold them back.

"I know I'm not supposed to see the bride before, but I'm going on the assumption that means only in the dress."

"I'll buy that." She smiled.

"I wanted to have a glass of champagne with you before we head down and you officially become my wife."

She couldn't speak so she nodded.

Warner walked to the table and opened the champagne with a pop of the cork. He poured them each a glass and then handed her one.

"Your hair and makeup look beautiful."

"Thank you. Thank you for all of this."

"I don't want you to regret a moment."

Clara thought about the conversation she'd had with her brother. She had regretted not telling anyone, but it had only lasted a moment. Warner was winning over those feelings. Everyone would know very soon.

Warner tapped his glass to hers. "This is to forever."

Her heart literally skipped a beat, she was sure of it as she steadied her breath trying to calm the thudding in her chest. "To forever."

They each sipped their drink.

Warner finally looked away from her and down to his watch. "Okay, it's time for you to get ready. Your dress is down in the dressing room in the chapel."

Clara placed her hand on her stomach. "Wow, we're really going to do this."

"You can still back out."

She shook her head. "No. It's not that easy to get rid of me, Mr. Wright." Just enough of the champagne had stirred in her that saying Mr. Wright made her giggle. He certainly was mister right.

"Good. I think Clara Wright has a wonderful ring to it."

"I do too."

He took her glass and set it on the table. "C'mon, my bride. I'll escort you downstairs."

CLARA'S DRESS HUNG IN THE ROOM. IT WASN'T FANCY AT ALL. IN fact, she'd picked one she could wear to almost any event. But it would be very special.

On the vanity there was a handwritten note from Warner. "Now we begin our forever."

She held the note to her chest. Marrying a man with a way with words would never get old, she was sure of that.

She took her phone out of her purse and took a few pictures of her dress and of the room. She knew they were going to have formal pictures, but she certainly wanted a few behind the scenes pictures to remember the day.

With ten minutes left before their seven o'clock wedding time, there was a knock at the door.

Clara opened the door to the photographer.

"I'd like to get a few shots of you in the chapel before the wedding."

Clara nodded and followed the woman down the hall.

She was impressed with the woman's efficiency, and she knew the album was going to be as spectacular as the wedding itself.

When it was time, Clara was escorted out of the room.

Witnesses were appointed to be at the wedding.

As the music started, one of the witnesses opened the chapel door and Clara walked down the aisle.

WARNER HAD THOUGHT HE'D LOST HIS HEART TO HER THE MOMENT he'd seen her at that stop light a few weeks ago. Then there was the moment when she'd kissed him and again when she'd said she loved him. But seeing Clara walk toward him in a simple, beautiful white dress—he was sure he'd died and gone to heaven.

When she reached him and she took his hand, he gazed into her eyes. "Wow. Just wow."

She smiled softly. "Thank you."

"I'm one lucky man."

"And I am one lucky woman."

The minister started the ceremony and Warner wasn't sure he heard one word the man said. It was a good thing it was being videotaped. Then he could relive it and he'd thought he'd only added on the video package to the wedding so that her parents could have a copy.

He did hear her loud and clear when she said, "I do," to the minister's question as to whether she'd be his bride.

It hadn't taken long, and soon the minister was telling him to kiss his bride.

No moment in his life had held more pride than that moment when he placed his hand on her cheek and pulled her in for the most romantic kiss they'd ever shared.

Whatever came his way for the rest of his life couldn't

possibly take away the joy he was feeling as his wife kissed him passionately.

He'd be a good husband and an attentive father, when the time came. But, out of sheer nerves, he knew he worried that Clara too would someday want to leave him.

CHAPTER 33

*C*lara figured no honeymoon would ever be long enough when a woman loved a man as fully as she loved her husband. Husband. That too would never grow old.

She kept her arms wrapped around his as they flew back to Nashville. There was going to be so much going on in the next few months, she just wanted to soak in every moment they'd have alone.

Warner was going to sign on to do the TV show, they were going to record his music and try and either sell it or get him signed, and she was going to need to decide on which career path she was going to take now. Realizing that her lead men were a full ten years younger than she was had hit her hard. And she wasn't sure she was ready to play the matronly roles yet. Though she'd toyed with telling Arianna that they should do Annie again, and this time she thought it would be fun to play Miss Hannigan.

The moment the plane landed in Nashville, both Clara and Warner reached for the phones and turned them back on. It was only a moment later that Clara's phone chimed with a text message.

"Who's looking for you?" Warner asked with a grin.

She looked at the screen. "Mom wants us over for dinner tonight."

"Do you think they know?"

After her conversation with her brother, she was sure they all did, though she never actually said she'd gotten married or planned too.

A moment later Warner's phone chimed a text message too.

Clara elbowed him playfully. "And who's looking for you?"

His brows knit as he looked at the screen. Then his lips pursed and his cheeks grew red.

"Warner, what's wrong?"

He rubbed his hand over his forehead. "We were sold out."

He held up his phone to her to see that Jeremy Smith had sent him a congratulations text and a video clip which had already hit the gossip shows. It was a clip from their wedding shot from the back of the chapel.

Clara let out a sigh. "I guess we know that my folks know now."

"He says Patricia was already interviewed by the local news and is playing up some sob story about me running away to get married and not even including her or my grandmother."

Clara dropped her shoulders. "Does she really think you'd invite her even if it had been a big event?"

He lifted his brows. "She's demented. She thinks I'm her kid or something. When I went over the other day to confront her…"

"You went to her house?"

"Yes."

"Why didn't you tell me this?"

"You had a show to do. I guess it slipped my mind."

Clara bit down on the inside of her cheek. He was her husband and they were still learning things about each other. She was going to have to deal with this and now his stepmother—ex-stepmother—was her problem too.

Then she thought more about what he'd said. "Your grand-mother is still alive?"

"Yes."

"I didn't know that either."

"Clara, I don't have anything to do with her. She did what she had to and when I was eighteen I had a one way ticket out the door. I already told you she dumped me off in Vegas with an aunt. She's no more my kin than my own mother."

The very comment stung. This man needed so much love. It was a good thing she came from a good home. Even though it wasn't going to be easy, and she could already tell that, she could give him that stable home he needed and deserved. But would he accept it?

ONCE THEY MADE IT THROUGH THE AIRPORT AND COLLECTED THEIR bags, they hurried to find Clara's Jeep. Clara wondered if he was aware of the man who had been following them since they'd collected their suitcases. But just as they threw the last bag into the car, Warner turned around and headed toward the man.

"What do you want?" His voice rose in anger and Clara kept her distance.

"I just wanted to ask you a few questions."

"Listen, pal. I don't have anything to share with you."

Warner turned around and headed back to the Jeep, but the man hadn't gone on. "Why did you elope?"

"None of your business."

"Is your wife pregnant?"

That stopped Warner in his tracks. He turned back to the man. "Who are you? I am no one you would be interested in."

"Sure. Everyone is interested in Patricia Little's son."

"I'm not her son. She's not my blood. I wish ya'll would just leave me the hell alone."

"But she owns Master Records now, how do you feel about that?"

He thought he just might be sick. That was why Jordan Farr was at her house.

"Listen, I had no future at Master Records. I guess she'll be making albums now. Good for her."

He turned around and walked back toward Clara. "I heard Savannah heard you sing."

Warner kept walking. "That one is public knowledge, pal."

He hurried and opened the door for Clara and shut it once she got in. She could hear the man rattle a few more questions off to him, but Warner ignored them.

This was going to be strange for her to get used to. Sure, she'd been giving interviews since she was thirteen about the shows they did at the theater, but no one had ever hunted her down. Then she felt the bead of sweat roll down the back of her neck. But someone once had. It felt like that night when she stood on that stage and knew someone was there. Someone who wanted to hurt her.

She tried to suck in a breath. She could still feel his hands on her covering her mouth. Never in her life had she been so afraid, but that night she thought she'd die.

Would Warner's unwanted fame bring those kind of people into their lives? What if he did sell and become a big name in the industry? What if Savannah really did want him to tour with her?

Clara's palms grew damp. She and Warner were crazy to put themselves out there so people could hurt them.

He reached over and touched her thigh. Her first reaction was to jump and he quickly retracted his hand.

"I'm sorry. That man has me worked up," she said.

"That's going to be the norm. Especially now that she has one more angle to hate me."

"Do reporters do that to you all the time? Just come after you like that?"

"More lately, now that I'm trying to get my music out there. I can't wait for her time in the lime light to be over. I have to move on or I have to move away. But if I'm not in Nashville, I'm not where I need to be."

He seemed to have a level head about it. She sure wished she did.

CHAPTER 34

*W*arner pulled her Jeep into the driveway and quickly hopped out to open her door. Clara had been quiet the whole ride home and he hoped that reporter, or stalker, didn't bother her that much. This was Nashville and they were moving themselves into the music industry. If everything worked out this would be the norm, and not just because Patricia Little had been married to his father and drove him to suicide.

As he opened the door his beautiful bride smiled at him. He took her hand and helped her out, capturing her in his arms and kissing her solidly on the lips.

"Mrs. Wright, we're home."

She rested her head against his chest. "I sure do like the sound of that."

"So do I." He took her hand and shut the door. "C'mon, I've been thinking about this for days now."

"What?" She was laughing as he led her across the front yard.

"I'm carrying you over the threshold of the house. That's what husbands do."

"Oh, Warner...I don't know about that."

He turned as they cleared the top step. "Well you either let me sweep you up off your feet in a romantic gesture or I throw you over my shoulder."

Now she was smiling that radiant smile and laughing. This was how it would be, he knew. His wife—their home—he was completely in love and this felt great.

He unlocked the door and pushed it open. "How is it going down, because I'm not kidding. I'll haul you in here."

She moved toward him and wrapped her arms around his neck. "I guess I'll give in to traditional. There has to be something we do that's traditional right?"

Warner smiled wide as he scooped up his bride. "Remember our wedding night? I do believe that is tradition."

A blush covered her cheeks. "That was just crazy love taking over."

"Hmm, well I'm thinking I could take you up on some crazy love right now."

"Then you'd better keep carrying me straight up those stairs."

He gave her a nod and a wink and did exactly that. There were a few hours before they were expected at her parents' house. That gave them a few hours to roll around in the sheets and enjoy one more day of their honeymoon.

WARNER PARKED CLARA'S JEEP IN FRONT OF HER PARENTS' HOUSE. Considering the driveway and the street was full, it looked like everyone had been invited. But only one person stood on the front porch, and that was her father.

"They know," he said through clenched teeth.

"I expect them to. Besides, they were going to find out tonight anyway."

"He's going to kill me."

Clara turned to face him. "He loves me. He wants to protect

me. You love me and you want the same. Don't assume the worst."

"I'm not trained to think any other way."

"Start." She leaned over and kissed him softly. "He'd be more shocked to find out I threw all your condoms in the trash."

"That was stupid on your part."

She laughed. "What's it worth to be married if you have to worry about it?" She gave him a wink and slid out of the Jeep.

Warner opened the door and let his foot touch the ground before he took in the deep breath he was going to need. Before he made it around the truck Carlos was headed toward them, and he wasn't smiling.

"Hi, Daddy." Clara moved toward him.

"I cannot believe you did this. I cannot believe you hurt your mother's feelings by running away," he said, fisting his hands on his hips.

"Dad, I'm thirty."

"And you've known him for three weeks," he said pointing to Warner.

Clara's hands fisted to her sides, just as her father had. "I'm happy. Would you wish that I was miserable and had waited?"

"No. Just some common courtesy to let us know where you'd gone."

Warner watched them interact, but he was surprised when Carlos was more upset about the trip than the wedding? He must not have heard that right.

"I left a note."

"A note that said you'd gone on vacation. C'mon, you could have gotten hurt or something could have happened, and we wouldn't have known where to find you."

She narrowed her eyes at her father. "I'm sorry."

Warner noticed there was a shimmer in Carlos's eyes. "I can't believe my baby got married."

Clara pulled Carlos in to her arms and hugged him tight. "I did. Oh, Daddy, I'm so happy."

"I knew you were." Carlos sniffed and pulled back from Clara and turned toward him. "You're going to take care of my baby, right?"

"Yes, sir. I love her very much."

"I know you do." He put his hand on Warner's shoulder. "You'll take good care of each other."

"I promise," Warner agreed and he hoped Carlos couldn't feel him shake under his hand.

"C'mon." Carlos wrapped his arm around Clara's shoulders. "There's a party happening inside. Darcy can't decide if she's happy for you or sad that you got married before she did, but she's happy for you."

"Ed's lucky to have her."

"We all are." Carlos gave Clara's arms a squeeze.

Warner began to follow them up the driveway and to the house. "Oh, I forgot the video. It's in the car. I'll be in in just a moment."

Clara nodded and walked through the door with her father and Warner hurried back to the Jeep to get the video.

He also had a little surprise in the glove compartment for Clara.

When he had the video in hand, and the small box, he headed back to the house as his phone rang. He looked at the screen to see the ID read Jeremy Smith.

"Hello."

"Congratulations! Had no idea that was going to happen."

"Yeah, kinda goes with the whole thought of eloping."

He slowed his walk as he approached the house.

"It sure will make for some interesting TV," Jeremy laughed, but Warner didn't like that. "Anyway, can you be in my office at ten tomorrow? The others who are doing the show will be here and we need to do some paperwork."

"Yeah, no problem."

"Great. And again, congratulations."

Warner tucked his phone into his pocket and walked into the house where the noise was nearly deafening.

He was greeted immediately by Darcy running to him and throwing her arms around him.

"God! I can't believe you took her and got married. That is so romantic!" She squealed in his ear.

As soon as Darcy let go of him her Aunt Simone swooped in. "I like your style." She kissed him on the cheek. "Curtis and I ran away too."

"And then she left me on a yacht," Curtis said as he slipped in behind his wife. "We got pregnant though." He narrowed his eyes on Warner.

"Oh, we just got married." He tried to smile though the fear that must have resonated in his voice.

Curtis laughed. "Congratulations."

He hadn't seen Clara in almost a half hour, by the time he was hugged and congratulated by the entire family. But it hadn't gone unnoticed that Madeline was the last to walk up to him.

"Congratulations, Warner." She kissed him hesitantly on the cheek.

"Thank you." He made sure to catch her eye as she nervously looked around the room. "I love her very much. I'm going to take good care of her."

Madeline let out a weak laugh. "Oh, honey, I think you're in for a shock if you think she needs taking care of."

"I didn't mean that she did. I mean that I will love her, comfort and protect her for the rest of my life. I hope I didn't offend you by getting married alone."

Madeline shook her head. "I mean, she is my only daughter. I won't lie that it stung a little."

"I understand. I do have something for you though."

He reached into his back pocket and pulled the CD case out.

"I had this made for you and Mr. Keller. She was so beautiful and the night was so magical. I knew she'd want to share it with you."

Madeline tucked in her lips and batted away the tears that were threatening to fall. "I saw her on TV. I know that the wedding was leaked out by someone, but I agree. She looked beautiful."

Warner pulled his new mother-in-law in for a hug and saw his wife smiling at him from across the room.

"Excuse me," he said softly to Madeline. "I have a gift for my beautiful wife."

He kissed his mother-in-law on the cheek and walked toward Clara.

"She's sad, isn't she?" Clara asked him.

"You're her only daughter."

"Damnit. I don't want her sad."

He caressed her cheek. "She's fine. Listen I have something for you."

Warner pulled the small box out of his pocket and handed it to her.

"What is this?"

"Open it."

Clara opened the small box and inside was a gold band etched with musical notes and a treble clef.

He took the ring out of the box. "I saw it when we landed in Nashville and since I didn't buy you a ring, I thought this would be a good starter for now."

He slid it on her finger and noticed that the room had gone silent.

"Warner, it's perfect."

"We make beautiful music together, and I don't just mean when we sing."

Clara wrapped her arms around his neck. "You're right. And no matter what we will always be in tune."

Warner kissed her softly. Who would have thought Warner Wright would have fallen into such a perfect moment in his life?

His phone buzzed in his pocket again, this time a text message.

Interesting move WW. Did you knock her up? Just like your daddy aren't you?

Clara held on to him, as she looked at her ring. "Who was that?"

"No one." And he truly meant it.

CHAPTER 35

*C*lara had taken her time rolling out of bed. Warner had already left for his meeting with Jeremy Smith.

Arianna had told Clara to take the week and enjoy her time as a newlywed, but she did expect her back as soon as the set was taken down. They had work to do. They always did a new talent showcase in November and that was coming up. And Clara had helped put the cast together for their next production, she had to be part of getting rehearsals together.

It was old hat, but a part of her longed to just follow Warner around and write songs with him. In time.

At ten-thirty her phone rang. She didn't recognize the phone number, but she never was one to let a call be missed.

"Hello."

"Clara Keller?" the man on the other end of the line asked.

"Yes."

"My name is Tom Wheeler. I represent Savannah."

Clara's hands shook. This was the call. This was Warner's turn at the big time. She'd heard his songs and now she wanted him. Why he was calling her, she had no clue. Perhaps he thought she represented him. In a way she did.

"Yes, sir. How are you?"

"I'm well thank you. I know this is short notice, but I was wondering if it would be possible to meet with you over lunch."

"I could make arrangements for that. What day are you looking at?" She was trying to sound as professional as she possibly could.

"Today at twelve. The Tavern on Broadway."

"Today?" She looked down at herself still in her lounge pants and tank top. "Sir, that would be fine. I'll be there at noon, but Warner is in a meeting today. I won't be able to bring him with me."

"Yes, we know. We want to meet with you."

The line went dead and Clara stood there and stared at the phone.

She was his wife and as such she would represent him the best she could. He was about to have his dreams come true.

WARNER SAT IN JEREMY SMITH'S OFFICE WITH THE OTHER PEOPLE that were featured on the TV show. There were two performers looking for recording contracts, three song writers looking to sell their music, and then there was Warner. They had made it clear they had wanted him for his writing talent, but now that they'd heard him, they thought that perhaps he would be perfect to spotlight with his performing too.

He'd cringed when he'd heard the name Patricia Little come up more than once, but he was going to keep his cool. Not one foul word was going to come from his lips in regards to the woman.

"We're going to get preliminary interviews done today with you all. You'll go into the studio and we will film you talking about your career and what you're looking to do here," Jeremy said from behind his massive desk. "We're going to embed you into the Nashville music scene and people are going to know who you are."

"Great. Are any of us going to get air time next to the stepchild of Cruella DeVille?" one of the others asked.

Warner's spine grew straighter, but Jeremy's hand came up. "Mr. Wright here is a very accomplished performer and song writer. Ms. Little's characterization on him is a little off balance."

"Doesn't matter. Seems to me he's going to get double the air time. Our show—her show."

Warner clenched his hands at his side in his chair.

Jeremy shook his head. "Show business, man. Nothing is fair."

They were dismissed, but Warner didn't like the way it all went down. Already there was a wall between him and the others. But what did it matter, right? Get his music out there and make it big, then he could treat Clara to the world. She deserved the world at her feet.

"Warner," Jeremy called him back to his desk. "Don't let them get to you. They know what kind of talent you have and their feelings are wearing on their sleeves."

Warner nodded. "As long as this show doesn't need me bad mouthing Patricia Little then we're fine. She has her demons to live with and I have a career to build."

A crooked grin formed on Jeremy's mouth. "High road, huh?"

"Best one, I figure."

"She bought out one of the leading record groups that we have looking at songs."

Warner shrugged. "I figure you knew that going in and you still wanted me here."

"I hold out that she's one serious pain in the ass. I don't like what she did to my show."

"Then don't make this one about her either. She'll eat it up if you do."

Jeremy nodded. "You're right. By the way, your new wife has

215

quite a talent of her own. Is that going to be a problem between you two?"

"Don't see how it could be. She's my partner in what we do."

"What if she breaks into the industry sooner than you do? I mean she has been performing in Nashville since she was thirteen."

Warner tucked his thumbs into his front pockets. "How many shows does this run? Ten?" Jeremy nodded. "I figure I've got one helluva shot. And if she's lucky enough to get a shot too, all the better. But I know that she's headed back to the theater next week to do what she loves to do. But all of this," he held up his hands as if the office encompassed all of Nashville, "comes second to my marriage."

"I like your style, Warner. Regardless of the success of this show, I think you're going to be just fine."

"I've been on my own most my life. It's nice to have a partner to go home to when the lights that are forced on you are turned off."

He left the office and headed for the studio. No matter what the man said, Warner still felt as though Jeremy Smith had hoped he'd roll over on Patricia Little. But if he was going to walk with the big boys in Nashville, he wasn't going to do it by smearing her name. She was doing a fine job all by herself.

CHAPTER 36

*C*lara had quickly showered and dressed as professionally as she could. Then she headed out the door toward Music Row.

As she parked, she took in the ambiance of one of the most famous areas in the nation. So much music had been recorded in this area and so many artists walked the streets. Others walked them too, hoping someday they'd be recording music. She'd never given thought to being a recording artist. Truly she'd only thought she'd sing on the stage at her aunt's theater. But singing on stage with Warner was a different feel. She loved the feeling of performing and the audience participating. And doing that with her husband was even better.

Husband. Oh how she loved that. She was Mrs. Warner Wright. Who would have thought that would have happened when he pulled up in that beat up truck and called out to her in the middle of the street?

TOM WHEELER WAS AN IMPRESSIVE LOOKING MAN WITH THE perfect hair and an expensive suit. Handsome by most standards, but Ed had been right, had Clara married a suit, she'd be miserable.

Tom stood as she approached the table. It was then that she realized he had been one of the people at the table with Savannah and Jeremy Smith when she and Warner performed the other night.

"I'm glad you could meet me on such short notice."

"My pleasure," Clara said sitting down across from the man.

He was easy at making small talk. They ordered their lunches and he had two more Jack and Cokes, but she'd assumed he'd already had a few.

She was half way through her lunch before Tom said, "Well, let's get down to why I asked you to meet me."

Good, she thought. It was time to represent Warner Wright— her husband. The thought made her smile.

"Jeremy had asked us to join him the other night when you and Mr. Wright performed."

"Warner, my husband."

Tom nodded. "I wasn't sure that was the truth. So you did get married, huh?"

"We sure did."

"Congratulations."

"Thank you."

He rubbed his chin and leaned in over the table. "This might make my proposition a little awkward." He sat back and sipped the last of his drink. "He's starting production on Jeremy's TV show, correct?"

"Yes, today was their first meeting. I haven't heard from him yet, but I assume he is still there."

Tom nodded as though he knew for a fact where Warner was. "Savannah was very impressed with the music you performed the other night."

"They were all originals from Warner."

"He certainly has a way with words, doesn't he?"

She thought about when she'd met him, it hadn't seemed as though he could even form a sentence then, but he was a master with words. "He most certainly is."

"He wouldn't have a problem letting you perform them, would he? Especially since you're married now?"

Clara dropped her hands to the napkin in her lap and gave it a little twist. "We performed his music just fine before we were married. I'm sure now that we are married we would perform the same music."

"No," he let out a little laugh. "I'm specifically saying I want you to perform his music."

Clara nodded slowly. "Me? Just me?"

"Savannah really liked your style. She thinks you would be perfect for her. She'd like to have you open for some of her shows on her current tour."

"Me?"

"Is there a problem?"

"Well, yes. No. I mean, I'm an actress."

"Yes, and you're an amazing vocal talent. She saw you performing on stage singing original material, and she likes you."

"But Warner?"

"This is the Woman On Top Tour. The only men on this tour are crew."

"Me?"

He signaled the waitress to bring him another drink. "You."

She hadn't been prepared for this. Where were the simple days of putting on a curly red wig and black Mary Janes?

Tom explained the logistics of the tour while he sipped on his new drink. Clara would be almost a side show act at ten of the thirty cities, but it did mean she'd be on the road for almost a month.

Clara kept checking her phone hoping Warner had responded to at least one of her text messages, but to no avail.

Tom's phone rang and he took the call. When he hung up he

signaled for the check. "Our star is done with her rehearsal. She wants to meet you."

"Today? I really would like to talk to my husband about this."

"Sometimes you have to make your own call," he said as he stood.

"When will I have to make my decision?" She gathered her purse and followed him out of the restaurant.

"Oh you're in or you're out. She needs to fill this spot on these tours. She likes you."

He was heading up the street. She assumed toward his office or to the studio where Savannah had rehearsed.

"I don't really understand this. I mean I was singing background to Warner. I didn't carry any of the songs."

"It seemed to do the job."

She checked her phone and sent Warner another text. This simply wasn't happening. How did her life get so complicated and full of amazing things in less than a month? But she'd considered doing this, hadn't she? There had been that spark when she performed Warner's song with Randy and she knew she'd wanted to do this. This was her opportunity.

Warner had his own opportunities brewing. The TV show was going to launch his career, so he would want her to be successful, right? This is what he would want for his wife.

CHAPTER 37

*W*arner was a quick study—and no one on this show liked him.

He'd already seen the attitude before him when the one guy, and he didn't remember his name because he just didn't care to, thought Warner would get more air time because of Patricia. The girl, who looked like she'd be better off singing in a tribute band to Metallica, had already been interviewed and he caught the part where she thought Warner's music was for sissies.

But what the hell did it really matter? Warner was looking to sell his songs and to get a contract. Heck, not everyone thought the world of Tim McGraw, George Strait, or even the OX. There were always going to be critics and this show was all about putting them together in a battle.

When Warner took his opportunity to be interviewed, the first question was about Patricia Little.

"Let's set the record straight," he said. "Patricia Little was unfortunately my step-mother from the time I was ten until I was twelve. I am in my thirties, and she's still a thorn in my side. So as far as I'm concerned, that can be your last question about Patricia

Little. She is nothing in my life and has nothing to do with my life."

"How about your new wife? That was sudden wasn't it?"

"Yeah. When you fall in love with the right girl, you marry her as fast as you can," Warner said with a smile.

"What about her career? She's going on tour, singing your songs. Does that make you feel like you've been left behind already?"

Warner narrowed his stare on the man behind the camera asking the questions. "What are you talking about?"

"She's meeting with Savannah's people right now. I'm sure you knew that."

Warner could feel the heat rise in his cheeks, and damn he was sure that showed on camera. He needed to control himself quickly or he was going to fall right into the trap of making himself look like an idiot on TV.

"My wife is a very talented woman. If Savannah liked her style then the woman has taste. As for her singing my songs, I can't think of anyone I'd rather have sing them."

The man nodded. Warner hadn't gotten all worked up. Their plan had failed—on camera at least. What the hell was Clara doing signing contracts to sing his songs?

He stood from the stool when the interview was over and headed right to the bathroom to splash cold water on his face. Well, he hadn't really expected his new wife to sell him out in only two days, but why would that differ from anyone else in his life?

Oh, she was going to get an earful when he got home. Maybe he had made a mistake running off and marrying her. After all, hadn't he assumed she was going to steal his songs anyway?

He reached into his pocket and turned on his phone to give her a call. He was curious as to what she would say to him.

Before he could dial the number the screen lit up with no less than ten text messages, notice of six missed calls, and a voice message.

He scanned through the texts.

Warner call me.

OMG Savannah wants me to sing with her. Call me.

Where are you?

I'm heading to her mgrs. office. They want me to contract.

Warner I need you.

Call me.

He let out a breath. She wasn't hiding from him. That stupid man who had interviewed him had inside knowledge of something and he was trying to use it against Warner. Well he was glad he'd played that off and they didn't get the fight they thought they would. Warner wasn't going to let this get to him. This was going to work for him, dammit!

Warner listened to the voice mail. The last one had only been sent fifteen minutes earlier.

"Warner, please call me as soon as you can." Clara sighed into the phone. "Savannah wants me to tour with her for ten cities. I'd be that act that goes out before anyone even gets into the arenas, but they want me to sing your songs. I need to know what you think. They want me to sign today or I'm out. I want to do this, but not without your consent. I'm in the bathroom now hoping you get this. Please call me or text me. I'm in Tom Wheeler's office down on Broadway. Please call me."

Warner felt his heart race. His Clara was going to sign a contract to perform his music. That stupid man had thought he'd get mad about that, but he wasn't. This was big for both of them.

He dialed Clara's number, but there was no answer. So he sent her a text.

You sign that contract and you make that woman proud. I'd be honored if you'd sing my songs.

He pushed send and waited a moment for her reply as he walked out to the hallway.

"Hey, Warner. I was looking for you," Jeremy said as he walked down the hall. "We're going to do some more camera shots of you all to get the opening shot."

"You guys are really pushing to do this fast, aren't you?"

"Keeps costs down."

"I see." Warner looked down at his phone as it buzzed in his hand.

Signed! I love you and we're going to be big!

He smiled as Jeremy looked over at him.

"Text from the wife?"

Warner nodded. "Yep, seems as though she just signed to tour with Savannah."

"Ya don't say?" Jeremy smiled.

"You might have given me some warning so I wouldn't look like an ass in that interview," Warner said.

"C'mon. It's all about reaction."

At that moment, Warner's reaction was to punch this guy in the gut. But that's what they wanted. They wanted to see how far this guy would go before he'd break like his father did. Well he had news for Nashville and the world—he wasn't going down like that. And they weren't going to pull his wife down either.

Warner thought about the tattoo on her wrist. The word "family" in the infinity symbol. They were family now, and a family stood together and fought together. He'd be damned if the need for good TV was based on him falling to pieces. Patricia Little could have all the bad press she wanted. He wasn't interested. What he was interested in was getting his music out there and it seemed as though Clara was doing just that.

They wanted good TV? They would get it. Only he wasn't going to say the woman's name aloud even once. He was going to write and perform and let Clara carry his music to the masses. She had ten show dates, he had ten episodes. In the end they'd still have each other. After all he was a Keller now, as she'd told him, and Kellers stuck together.

Oh, Jeremy Smith thought he'd get some dirt because he too despised Patricia Little. Patty was going to work any angle she could to show the world Warner now could fail on TV and in anything he did. But they were going to be disappointed. Mr. and Mrs. Wright were going to ride this to the top.

Warner walked into the studio where the others from the show had been waiting. Kill 'em with kindness, he thought and gave everyone a big smile. "Let's get this show on the road. I got a wife with a touring contract to get home to."

CHAPTER 38

*I*t was nearly seven o'clock before Warner made it home. The only person there was Christian. He'd really hoped to have a few moments to talk to his wife, but she hadn't answered his call on the drive home or any of his texts in the past hour.

So much had happened in one day and it wasn't until he was alone in his truck, with the radio off, and nothing but the sound of traffic on the street that he realized all of this was too coincidental.

Three weeks ago he was being told he had no talent. Jordan Farr had given him a little hope and then Warner found him at Patty's house. Now Patty owned part of the record label most likely to ever sign him.

He gets a gig to play in front of someone, whom he now knew was Savannah. Suddenly he's signed to do ten episodes of some TV reality show and his wife, who only sang backup to him and Randy, except for once when she sang his song, now was going to tour with Savannah. None of this made sense and at the same time, wasn't it what they wanted?

Warner pushed open the back door and Christian was at the kitchen table. He looked up at him.

"Hey."

Warner shut the door. "Hey."

"Clara's not with you?"

He set his keys on the counter. "No. She's got something going on."

Christian nodded his head. "Was just hoping to talk to her. I need her opinion."

"Anything I can help with?"

Christian winced, though Warner wasn't sure he knew he had, but then he nodded. "Maybe. You've been through this already." Christian pushed a small box to the middle of the table. "What do you think?"

Warner walked over to the box. It was a ring box. He opened it slowly revealing the biggest solitaire Warner had ever seen, and he knew Patricia Little's taste in fine jewelry.

"Please don't let my wife see this. I can't afford one of these."

Christian laughed a nervous laugh. "It's nice, huh?"

"Gorgeous."

"Yeah, I'm hoping it'll do the trick. I'm going to ask Tori to marry me."

Warner smiled. "Trust me. If she loves you, the ring will be only the icing on the cake, not the reason."

"I know. I know. It's just," he let out a breath, "I'm nervous."

Warner knew what he meant. He'd been nervous too, but it worked out to his benefit. He was married to Clara and even though they were still learning about each other, he couldn't imagine that years of waiting would have made it any better.

"When are you going to ask her?"

Christian bit down on his lip. "I don't know exactly. I keep thinking I want to plan it all out, every moment of the night. But then I keep thinking spontaneous is better, right?"

"It worked for me."

"Yeah." Christian picked up the ring and looked it over. "Maybe that'll be best. Spontaneous."

"You'll know when it's right."

Christian looked up at him. "What made you do it? I mean why marry someone when you've only met them? Aren't you worried the Kellers are crazy and now you're caught up in it?"

That made Warner laugh hard. "Are you kidding me? My mother left when I was ten because she was tired of being a mom. My dad committed suicide after his wife ran off on him and she went on to ruin the career of the OX. And she has spent the rest of the time trying to ruin me, although I don't know why. My grandmother disliked me as much as my mother did and she shipped me off to Vegas to live with some aunt for a while. I'm thinking any crazy in this family is welcomed."

"Damn. I thought getting injured and losing my career was bad."

"Don't think I'm looking for sympathy. Not everyone has a family like yours. Even though your parents had a hard time, you were still taken care of."

Christian nodded. "Yeah, even when Mom was married to Matt things were good."

"Not many kids get their wish that their parents get back together."

"True. I know this sounds bad, but sometimes I think the best thing to happen to us all was Mom's cancer."

"It brought you all together."

Christian looked at the ring again and began to laugh. "I remember coming home from school and you could hear laughing from the bathroom. And there was Mom with her head shaved and she was shaving Dad's head."

Warner smiled. "That's commitment."

"Oh, his fiancée was mad. But he did it to comfort Mom. Then Ed sat down and shaved his head too."

"What about you?"

The smile left Christian's face. "Nah, I was too scared back then. I was afraid of everything, especially losing Mom. Clara and I ran the opposite direction when he offered to shave our heads."

That made Warner laugh again. Just the image in his head of the two of them turning tail.

Christian took the ring out of the box and rolled it between his fingers. "There are nights I lie awake wishing I'd joined them. I was selfish not to."

"You can't regret it."

"I know. But think about it, if it happened now, both Clara and I would be first in line."

Warner widened his stare at his brother-in-law. "Damn, she totally would too."

Christian laughed. "I know, right?"

The back door opened and Clara walked in looking more than a little frazzled.

"Hey, sweetheart," Warner said as he walked to her and pulled her into him tightly.

"Hey." She set her keys next to his on the counter and dropped her purse on the floor. "What are you boys doing?"

"Christian was asking for fashion advice," Warner grinned.

"Fashion advice? Are you over the basketball shorts and T-shirt stage?"

"Ha, ha very funny," Christian stood and walked toward her. "This guy's opinion on this was exactly what I needed. But I'll show you too."

He opened the box in his hand and showed her the ring.

Clara cupped her hands over her mouth. "Oh, Chris, it's beautiful."

"It is, isn't it?"

"You're going to ask her? You're really going to do this?"

"I didn't expect my little sister to beat me to the altar." He winked at her when she gave him an irritated sister look. "I'm ready. I have the house. I have the ring. I almost have all the time in the world since I'm not going to play next year."

"She's a lucky girl."

"I know."

Clara laughed and slapped Christian on the arm. "I'm lucky too. Tori and Darcy for sisters. I won the lottery."

"I'll tell her you said that." He ran his hand over his unshaven chin. "I guess I'd better go get a shower. She's having me over for dinner with her parents. Her sister and Dave will be there with their kids. I guess if the mood hits me I'll ask her to marry me. If I'm scared to death I'll come home with this ring."

Clara moved in and hugged her brother. "You deserve this. Don't back out."

"I'll let you know how it goes." He gave them both a nod and left the kitchen.

CHAPTER 39

Clara dropped her shoulders and turned to Warner. "Long day, huh?"

"Sure was," he said pulling her to him. "Congratulations."

"To you too."

"So what is she like? Savannah? I hear she's the biggest country diva we have."

Clara laughed as she rested her hands on her husband's chest. "I'm not even sure she's country. One minute she's Shania Twain and the next she's Lady GaGa."

He laughed at that. "That's what I've heard."

Clara turned and walked toward the table. She didn't sit down, but stood behind a chair with her hands on the back it. "But why me? None of this makes sense."

"Because this is how the industry works."

"No. Not like this." She pulled her hair through her hands and let it fall. "I found out she did hear me when I played with Randy. The night I sang your song."

"That makes me feel better about it."

"But other than on stage, I'm backup. C'mon you're not going to sign someone who spent the last two month singing West Side Story."

"But they did."

"And they want me to sing your songs."

He smiled. "That was the point right? You'd sing my songs and we'd sell them?"

"Right, but," she gritted her teeth, "it still doesn't make sense."

Warner walked to her and put his hands on her hips, making her turn toward him. "Somewhere, someone is trying to see what kind of trouble we can get into. We've only fueled the fire by running off and getting married. The odds are against us."

"What are you saying?"

Warner pulled out his phone and clicked on the browser. He enlarged the screen. "I did some digging at the stoplight on my way home."

He handed her the phone.

"Oh."

"Yeah. Our Savannah is signed by Jordan Farr."

"Master Records."

"Patricia Little's newest financial gain."

She handed him the phone back. "I don't understand any of this. Why does a woman who left your father and you after two years still hold this grudge?"

Warner stepped back and ran his fingers through his hair. He turned and looked out the window.

"Warner," she said with her voice quivering.

"Clara, everything in my life has been ugly until you came along. You know that? Everything."

"Warner, what is it you're not telling me?"

He paced the kitchen floor and Clara's heart began to race. What secrets did he have? Who was this man she'd married?

Warner paced some more and Clara finally stepped in front of him. "You are hiding something from me. Now spill it or get the hell out of my house."

He stopped pacing and she could see the vein at his temple pulse.

"You're like everyone else, huh? Warner needs a moment and you turn on him?"

"I don't do secrets."

"And I don't do bullying."

Clara stepped up closer to him. "I'm not bullying you. I'm trying to get my answer. My husband is hiding something from me."

"He's not hiding it," he said and his voice softened. "He just doesn't know how to tell you."

Her heart rate kicked up even harder.

"You're scaring me."

He turned toward her, but he took a step back from her and not closer to her.

"Patty had a daughter. She was two years older than me." He turned and placed his hands on the counter top and bowed his head. "Patty never had much to do with her. I only met her a few times while she was even married to my dad." He sucked in a long, deep breath and let it out. "She hated Patty as much as I did."

Clara felt her stomach twist. She didn't want to hear about another woman. She didn't want to know anything about Warner loving someone else, but she felt it coming. Why else would he mention her?

"When I was about fourteen I had decided that I was already too good for school and the day was better drinking behind the gym shed. I was usually drunk and passed out by the time my grandma got home. Drinking led to pot. Pot led to…"

Clara couldn't help but gasp and Warner turned his head.

"You want me to stop?"

She shook her head, urging him to continue, but she wasn't sure she wanted him to.

He turned and backed against the counter shoving his hands into his front pockets.

"I was at this party one night and my buddy brought this girl with him. I was trashed and she made me look sober. I didn't recognize her, Clara." He looked up at her. "It was Mindy and I had no idea."

"Mindy? Patricia Little's daughter?"

"Yeah." He stepped away from the counter and walked to the table where he stood as she had earlier with his hands on the back of the chair. "We both ended up sleeping the night off on the guy's couch. She knew who I was right away. She acted like I was the long lost piece of her life."

Clara watched him search for the rest of his story. She wanted to stop him from continuing. It already hurt too much to find out who he really was.

"You and Mindy?"

"Me and Mindy." He pulled the chair out and sat down. He clasped his hands on lap and hung his head. "When Patty and my grandma found out we were—well you know—Grandma shipped me off to Vegas to live with my aunt."

"You were so young."

"I was. Seems so long ago." He sat up and pressed his back to the chair. "Anyway, sending a kid to the cesspool of Vegas when he already has a drinking problem and a drug addiction isn't the smartest thing. But I was there for the next year or so. I made some friends. I was even in a band." He laughed. "They'd sneak me into bars because I wasn't old enough to be in the bar I was playing in."

"How old were they?"

"Old enough."

Clara realized her own hands shook as he continued his story, so she tucked them behind her.

"Anyway, I was just another low life on the streets of Vegas. My aunt usually didn't know where I was or care. Then one day

Mindy walks through the door. It was like my salvation. There was my woman."

Clara thought she was going to be ill.

"She'd hitched a ride when she found out where I was. She was almost eighteen now. The guy she'd hitched a ride from had driven her for a few rounds in the back seat."

"Oh, Warner. That's horrible."

"This was life, Clara. This was the norm. We didn't have this perfect protected life you did."

"And you're holding that against me?"

"No, but it sounds like you're holding it against me."

CHAPTER 40

$\mathcal{H}$e was right. She wouldn't have married him if she thought he was bad for her. But she certainly hadn't expected this.

"Mindy and I fell right back into our routine. Then she started collecting men. I was just who she ran back to when she had used them up to get what she wanted. I was young, but I had feelings. I didn't want to just be her guy for sex or the connection for her drugs."

"Warner, this is killing me." Clara walked out of the kitchen and into the living room.

"Let me finish and then I'll go."

"You'll go?"

"You can't even hear the rest of my story without walking away from me. Clara, this is the way it works in my life. People find out who I was and they walk. I'm prepared for you to do the same."

"I'm not like everyone else."

"Then prove it and sit down and listen to me."

Clara felt as though he'd kicked her in the gut. And worse, she deserved his anger.

She sat down and he continued.

"Anyway, I decided I needed to stop the drinking and the drugs. I was much too young to be having a woman in my bed when I woke up, especially one who was continually trashed. So I stopped doing drugs and eventually stopped drinking. I saved up enough money for a bus ticket to Nashville and one night I told her I was going home."

"She didn't want to come with you?"

"No. Her kind of life was right there. She threw the biggest fit I'd ever seen a woman throw, and mind you I was there when her mother threw some serious fits. But she got a few punches in on me. Blacked my eye and bloodied my nose. She even cracked a rib. I got on the bus and she went back to whatever guy she'd been with the night before and…"

He shook his head, swallowed hard, and rubbed his hand over the back of his neck. "Well they tied on the worst concoction of coke and booze ever. But I don't think that was all."

Warner stood, walked toward the window, and looked out over the yard. "Patty found out I was back in town and she came after me with a vengeance. She wanted to know where her daughter was and I told her. I looked her right in the eye, with my black one that Mindy had given me, and told her that her daughter was turning tricks in Vegas for drugs and booze."

"What did she say to that?"

"She called me a liar. Said that if that was true, I must have been the one that put her up to it."

"She didn't know her own daughter well enough to know what kind of person she was?"

"She'd never admit it."

Clara wrung her hands together. "Did she find her?"

Warner walked back to the table and sat down. "She found her. She was marked as a Jane Doe in the morgue. That last night of partying was the last one forever. The guy she'd run back to was arrested for her death."

Sickness swam in Clara's stomach. "So Patricia knows you had nothing to do with that."

"She knows, but she still holds me accountable. She thinks I'm the one who started her drug addiction and drinking. She assumes that I asked Mindy to go to Las Vegas. And she will keep to her promise to ruin everything I ever try to do. Look at my teaching jobs, my performing opportunities, the only alliance I had at a record company."

"Warner this was nearly fifteen years ago. She needs to let it go."

"She's not going to. Mindy was her daughter. Now Patricia is thriving on taking me down."

"We have to make her stop. I have to get out of this contract on this tour. I can't work on something with my heart when I know she's behind it."

Warner shook his head. "First of all, you don't get out of contracts." He chuckled, then looked back down at his hands. "I think it's possible to make this work in our benefit. I really do."

"Take the high road?"

"Right." He finally turned his head and looked at her. He tucked his lips between his teeth and let his shoulders drop. "You have full access to my catalog of songs."

"Thank you."

"We're married. What's mine is yours. I'll even sign over the rights if you need me to."

"I don't think that's necessary."

He swallowed hard. "And now I'll go pack my things."

Clara felt her jaw tighten. "You'll what?"

"I just dumped a whole lot of undesirable information on you. I'd understand if you needed some time to sort out who you just married."

"I've seen you drink one beer since we've been together."

"Yes."

"I've been in the entertainment industry long enough to know if you're gay or stoned, and neither seem to be the case."

He chuckled again. "I'm not stoned or gay."

"You're clean, right?"

"Since I left Vegas that day."

She felt her cheek twitch and she knew Warner saw it. There was doubt brewing in her and she hated that. He was willing to leave and she was the one holding him back from doing so. But she loved him and if she'd learned anything from being a Keller; it was that love always won.

"You'll stay here. You're my husband and I love you."

"You didn't know about my past. You didn't know about Mindy."

Clara shot her shoulders back and straightened her spine. "Fine, would you like to hear about my love affairs?"

Warner shook his head and smiled. "No. I really wouldn't like to hear that."

"Good, because I don't want to talk about them." She leaned in closer to him and took his hands in hers. "The worst thing to ever happen to me was my mom's cancer and Michael Hamilton trying to kill me."

Warner lifted his hand to her cheek. "Oh, is that all?"

Clara let down her guard. "Yeah, that's all. We can work through all of this. She can't destroy you forever."

"She'll try."

"And I'll be here. I've got your back."

"I love you, Mrs. Wright."

"Back atcha, Mr. Wright."

CHAPTER 41

*C*lara believed every word her husband told her, but still she was sitting in the chair in the corner of their bedroom at two in the morning contemplating it all. Warner slept peacefully and Clara hadn't gotten a wink of sleep.

Who was this man she married? His family was gone—that was the only way to look at it. How could a mother hate her child and turn him away? What made Patricia Little neglect her own daughter?

How could a grandmother send her grandson away and a father think it would be better if he were dead? None of this made sense to her.

Warner rolled over and Clara sucked in a breath and sat still. She didn't want to talk to him anymore tonight. She was afraid, perhaps, there was more.

The thought of the young love affair with Mindy had her sick to her stomach. When she was fourteen her parents were happily married again and her mother was in remission. Sure, she had her one demon, but she was in the wrong place at the wrong time and she knew that.

Warner's life sounded like it had all been times of wrong timing in wrong places.

She could let go the affair with Patricia's daughter. What boy at that age wouldn't have loved to have had an older girl want him at all times? But the drugs and the alcohol—she couldn't wrap her head around it.

Was there a turning point back to that? What if he did sign a recording deal and he ended up on tour? There would be lots of booze, drugs, and women.

Clara tried to let out a calming breath. She seriously thought she was going to be sick.

It was then she decided sleep wasn't going to happen and she'd go to the kitchen and get a glass of water.

As she filled her glass she heard footsteps on the stairs. From their rhythm she knew they were Christian's. His limp gave him away.

"Hey," he said softly from the living room.

"Hey."

"You okay?" He walked into the kitchen and pulled down his own glass from the cupboard and filled it with water.

"Yeah. I'm fine."

"You have a lot to think about, huh?"

Clara dropped her shoulders and rolled her head to release the tension in her neck. "You heard all of that?"

"I heard." He set his glass on the counter and turned to her in the moonlight. "What are you going to do? You don't really know this guy."

"This guy is my husband."

"Who you ran off and married without telling anyone."

"That's what elopement is all about." Her whisper was growing in volume.

"I'm scared for you. What if he still does drugs and you don't know? What if that girl gave him some disease?"

"Dear Lord, did you hear everything."

"This house isn't that big you know."

Clara paced the kitchen floor. "I love him, Chris. I love him so much. I have to think beyond all of this and accept that he's not that same man. I mean look, he got a job and put himself through college. He has two different degrees. What kind of druggie does that?"

"I'm just worried for you. I mean don't get me wrong, I like the guy." He lifted his hands in the air and let them drop. "You're my little sister. I'm supposed to think no one is good enough for you."

"I know. But I married him and he needs me in more than one way. He needs all of us. He needs the Kellers. He needs that love, that strength, he needs family."

Christian nodded. "I couldn't agree with you more." He walked toward Clara and pulled her into a hug. "You have a huge support group. Don't let us all down by not using us if you need us."

Clara only nodded.

Christian let go and headed back for the stairs. "Oh, by the way, congrats on the tour."

"Thanks."

"Can you get me Savannah's autograph?"

She snorted out a laugh. "I'll see what I can do."

CLARA WAS CONVENIENTLY GONE BEFORE WARNER WOKE UP. SHE had to be in Tom Wheeler's office by noon and she had rehearsals all afternoon.

She had rummaged through Warner's music and taken the pieces she liked best. It felt wrong to her, as if she were stealing them. But she left a note and a list. She was going to take them by the office supply store and have copies made first. She didn't want anyone else stealing them either.

But before she dealt with her new found music career, she

needed to talk to someone. She'd called Darcy and asked her to meet her at the Starbucks.

After all, Darcy was as close to a sister as Clara had.

Darcy was already getting her drink at the counter when Clara walked in.

"I got yours," Darcy called across the store and those in line watched her retrieve her drinks.

"Thank you." Clara took the cup and carefully sipped.

"Do you want to go upstairs and talk in the board room?"

"No," she was quick to answer.

"Oh, private conversation, huh? I love our sister time." Darcy giggled and found them a table.

They both sat down and arranged their purses and jackets.

Darcy lifted her cup to her lips and peered at Clara from over the top. "Okay. So what's the news? Are you pregnant already?"

Clara shook her head. "No, there's no baby." Hadn't that been on her mind too? She already had put a call into the doctor to get her back on the pill. She had been very optimistic and sure of herself the other night when she made a scene throwing out his condoms. But now, any little mishap—welcomed or not—wasn't even something she wanted to think about.

Darcy blew out a breath. "I don't want to sound petty, but I'm glad. I didn't know how I was going to react if you got married and pregnant before me. But that sounds even more petty. Pretend like I didn't say anything."

Clara smiled. She understood Darcy's dilemma, petty or not.

Darcy lifted her drink to her lips. "So, what's up?"

Clara dove into Warner's story, leaving no detail out. And when she was done she sat back in her chair and watched for Darcy's reaction.

"You're thinking about leaving him, aren't you?" The question was posed, but Darcy sounded angry.

"No. Well—I don't know. I don't know what to do."

"I should throw this coffee on you and wake you up."

"What?" That certainly wasn't what Clara expected.

"You're judging him by the circumstances in which he was raised."

Clara sunk into her chair and listened.

"You were born to a mother and father who loved you very much. Even when they weren't together, your step-father loved you and your parents were always around. You have aunts and uncles who love you, and your grandparents are like no others. But what if—just what if your mom and dad didn't work out again? What if Matt was an ass who beat you or worse? What if Arianna didn't have her theater and didn't care that you had talent? Then what?"

Clara's palms were sweating. She didn't like this.

Darcy continued, "Imagine not knowing the people you called mom and dad all your life weren't yours. Can you even imagine that?"

"Darcy, I didn't mean..."

"No. You didn't mean anything by it. But I know now what it's like to have someone's blood run through your veins that everyone hates. My biological father tried to kill you. Do you think about that when you think about that night? No. You probably don't associate that at all. I'm your sister. He was a monster. Who would I have been had he not tried to kill me and Regan before I was born?"

Clara covered her mouth forcing back the sob she wanted to let free.

"Clara, who you are at fourteen, or eighteen, doesn't define who you become. He's clean. I can tell he's not hiding anything from you like that. And he gave you all his music, right? You are now the artist of that music and he can't sell it on his show. He has to come up with new stuff. That was unselfish on his part."

"Oh, Darcy, what did I do?"

"You took an opportunity. Now go make something of it. I

want to meet Blake Shelton and until you get into that crowd I'm not going to."

Clara laughed a loud. "I love you. I'm glad that goofball brother of mine has you."

"Yes, yes. You're all lucky I came here looking for my missing piece. Now, I have a boring meeting with Zach and Ed. So I have to go back upstairs now. You go fix your marriage."

Clara stood when Darcy stood and gave her a hug. She'd put her marriage back together after she rehearsed her stolen songs.

CHAPTER 42

*B*eginning tomorrow, Warner would have cameras following him three days a week. For today, he was going to spend his time in his "studio" in the basement working on music.

He figured, as he wrote down the chords he'd just put together on the sheet music, that Clara leaving so early in the morning without waking him wasn't a good sign.

He'd texted her a few times, but she hadn't returned them.

How could he blame her? He'd dropped a heavy load on her last night and expected her to just understand. The good sign had been that his bags hadn't been packed and by the door.

When he heard footsteps upstairs he checked his watch. It was already six o'clock. But there were more than one set of footsteps. There were many and they were coming down the stairs to the small apartment in the basement.

Warner put his guitar on the stand and walked out into the hallway. Walking through the door were a lot of Keller men. Ed, Christian, Spencer, John, Zach, and even Carlos.

"Hey guys," he said and he hoped they didn't hear the fear in his voice. Had she sent her hit men to take him out?

Ed stepped forward. "Rumor has it you have the night free."

"I do?"

Christian laughed. "Your wife said so."

"Oh." Again he was sure they wouldn't beat him, but help throw his stuff in the truck—yeah.

Ed stepped closer to him. "See, there's only one problem with running off and getting married so quickly."

"Only one?"

Ed smiled as he rested his hand on Warner's shoulder. "You didn't get a bachelor party."

His breath of relief must have been so audible that even Carlos had smiled. Family—he was going to have to get used to it.

As bachelor parties went, Warner figured this one to be tame. They ended up at a sports bar on Music Row. He too wondered how planned that was.

There was a huge table by the bar reserved for them. Someone had already ordered platters of wings and fries and pitchers of soda. Obviously word had gotten out about his past— or so he would assume, otherwise he had to figure those pitchers would have been full of beer.

It didn't matter. These men were there to take him out and accept him as one of their own. This was a blessing. If he made it home without any of them beating him in the parking lot, and his wife was there, he figured they'd be okay—forever.

Carlos was the first to fill his plate with wings. "So, Warner, tell us about this TV show you're on."

"Oh, well, it will be interesting. I think he's thinking of me more as a performer than a song writer. But now with Clara performing my songs, I really don't know what they will be doing with me. I mean the purpose was to get the artists and their music found."

"It certainly sounds interesting. And Clara will be traveling?"

"Ten cities."

"My baby is a performer." He smiled. "We're pretty proud."

"I'm proud of her too."

Zach was the next to fill his plate. "I heard a new recording company is starting up soon. We were just approached for a bid to design. New building with studios."

That had Warner's attention. "Who's heading that up?"

"It was a group, can't say I know any specific names."

At least it was promising, he thought.

The conversation was good and that was what Warner needed most. There was no doubt these men knew his story but not one of them seem to judge him. As the evening progressed, one by one each man left after giving Warner a pat on the back and their own words of congratulations. Eventually it was Carlos and Warner left at the table. Warner was sure this was by design.

The waitress approached the table and told Carlos that the bill has been taken care of by Zach. Carlos shook his head and laughed. "That man never ceases to amaze me. He's taken care of a lot of us over the years." Carlos took a sip of his drink and set it back on the table. "He knew I set this up and was going to pay for it. I don't know why he does that. He's just that kind of a guy."

Warner shifted in his chair. "You set this up?"

Carlos nodded. "Yes. You needed a night out with the guys, and we needed to celebrate your marriage, like men."

Warner laughed. "I appreciate it more than you know."

"It sounds like things haven't been easy for you. I know that's hard. Clara won't give up on you. She's not made like that."

"I hope you're right. I love her more than I thought I could love anybody. And I'm not just saying that because you're her father. It's true. Fate stepped in at the right time. Though I have to admit I didn't expect any of this. The marriage. The show. Her singing my music. Or gaining a family."

Carlos leaned on the table with his elbows. The look on his face said that he was contemplating his words. "I didn't know I was giving my blessing for a wedding when you and I last spoke. But I think she did good with you. Not everybody gets to choose how they start life. We get to choose how we live our life. You seem to have made the right choices."

Warner wasn't the kind of man to cry, especially in front of another man. But he could feel the tears well in his eyes and sting in his throat. "I just wish mistakes from your childhood didn't have to follow you into adulthood. I'm more than what I was when I was a teenager. Things would be different had that have been different."

"You can't change that. It's time to move on. And something tells me things are going to go your way very soon."

"What makes you say that?"

"You're married to my daughter. She gets what she wants out of life. And she wants you and your success. Like I said, everything is going to be fine."

Warner bit down on his lip. The tears were stinging harder in his eyes. "I think you're right. As a team I think we can conquer anything. We will just have to get past these few weeks, even months, until we can move forward together."

"Let me ask, because it wouldn't be a fatherly thing if I didn't, what are your plans if your music doesn't take off?"

"I would go back into teaching," Warner said without hesitation. "I enjoyed the kids and seeing what they could learn. I truly think that's where my calling is, aside from writing music."

Carlos smiled wide. "I totally understand that. I don't know what I would have done all those years had I not been teaching. The administrative side was a whole lot different. The magic is in the classroom. Those kids are yours to mold, to shape the future. I think you'd be a fine teacher."

Warner cleared his throat. "Thank you for that. That means a lot."

"You'd better get home to your wife then. She'll be looking for you soon."

"Thank you for the night out. It was unexpected and very nice."

"You're one of us now. We're a support system for each other. The women in this family, well, they come with a support group."

Warner laughed. He supposed that was true enough. From what he could tell already, the Keller women were a strong breed. And those other women who joined the clan, well they were just as strong. The men in this family would have to be a good alliance for their women and for themselves. But he was part of a family now. And families stuck together—especially this one.

CHAPTER 43

*T*he following week was filled with rehearsals for Clara. She was all of twenty minutes of the concert, for only a few dates, and she couldn't believe how much time she'd already put into practicing everything.

She wasn't sure it was in her to be a headliner.

Things at home had been calm, and for that she was thankful. After her father's impromptu bachelor party for Warner, she'd noticed a change in her husband. It was almost as if he had new purpose in his life.

There were a few days a week he stayed purposely away from home since the cameras were following him for his show. She didn't mind that. Her tour schedule didn't need to affect his TV schedule, or what they put on TV for that matter.

Clara sat in the back of the room where the other small opening act was rehearsing. She liked being around like minded people and she knew Warner wouldn't be home until long after ten o'clock, so she saw no reason not to sit around and collaborate with the others she'd be touring with.

Trent Post, the guitarist for the other group, which called

themselves The Broke Tourists, walked toward her, his guitar in his hand being held by the neck.

"What do you think so far?"

Clara looked up at him. "You guys sound great."

Trent sat down on the folding chair next to her. "No. I mean about doing the tour and all. Savannah is a hard ass, isn't she?"

Clara smiled as she balanced her guitar on her knee. "A tour this big, you'd have a lot at stake."

"I guess it'll be our turn someday. I mean that's the reason we're doing this, right? So that the ticket stubs have our names on them."

"Something like that." She went back to tuning her guitar.

Trent looked around the room and Clara assumed he had more to say to her. She looked back up and caught his eye.

"So someone said you just got married?"

Clara nodded. "I sure did."

"Yeah, me too. She's a little freaked out about me being on the road so much. What about your husband?"

"He hasn't mentioned anything about it. He's excited for me. After all, I'm singing his songs."

"Right. He wrote all of those?"

"Yep."

"Talented S.O.B."

That made Clara laugh. "He sure is."

"He's that step-son of that gal on that reality TV show right? Nashville Ex-wives?"

Clara felt her throat go dry. "Yes, that's him."

Trent leaned in closer to Clara. "She's a bitch. I don't know how he deals with that."

"He doesn't," she said softly back. "She does it for publicity. She has nothing to do with him."

Trent nodded. "I'm surprised she let you on the tour since Savannah is signed under her label."

"I figure she's waiting for me to make a mistake." Clara set her guitar up on its end. "I won't be making any mistakes."

Trent smiled. "I think we're going to have a lot of fun on the tour. I'm glad you're on it."

"So am I."

WHEN CLARA PULLED INTO THE DRIVEWAY SHE HAD ONLY ONE THING on her mind—sleep. She hopped out of the Jeep and headed to the door when Warner's truck sped up the street. He stopped quickly in front of the house, jammed the truck into park, and jumped out.

"Are you okay?" Clara was headed toward him, but he was barreling at her as quickly as possible.

It was dark in the yard but that didn't hide the fact that his lip was bleeding, his eye was black, and his shirt was ripped.

"Warner, what happened to you? Oh, God, are you alright?" She dropped her bag and guitar case right where she stood and hurried to him.

She reached for his face but he pushed her hands away. "Don't touch it."

"Warner, that needs stitches."

"Like hell it does. It needs an icepack."

He moved around her and up the front steps.

Clara didn't even reach for her belongings. She followed him right into the house. "Who did that to you?"

"Not important."

"Like hell it's not." She followed him into the kitchen as he pulled a towel out of the drawer and walked to the freezer.

Clara moved in and took the towel from his hand and filled it with ice. "Sweetheart, what's going on? Why did someone do this to you?"

"Why? Because I'm a joke, Clara. I'm one big joke in this town."

"That's crap and you know it."

"Really? Tell that to those guys on my show. Stupid Patty mentions my name on her show last night, which by the way was taped weeks ago because there is footage of me leaving her house. I haven't been there since before we were married." He winced when she pressed the towel to his cheek. "She made her usual snide comments about me, but they are bent out of shape thinking I'm taking over the show. I'm getting double the air time thanks to that bitch."

"Warner, that's not how this is. We have to get you off the show."

"That's not going to happen. Just like pulling you off that tour isn't going to happen."

She felt the pang of losing her opportunity when he said that. Oh, she wished it wasn't like this. Warner should be with her on the road and not home doing this stupid TV show. But she kept in mind that by spring this would all be over.

Her tour dates would be over and his filming schedule would be done. At some point they could settle into being Mr. and Mrs. Wright.

Another car pulled up in the front and the driver parked and hurried out of the car. Again she could tell it was Christian by the sound.

The front door opened and Christian and Victoria flew into the room.

"What's wrong? Why does Warner's truck have a broken back window and all your stuff is outside on the ground?" Christian looked from her to Warner. "Christ! Clara, what did you do?"

"Me?"

She saw Warner's mouth lift into a smile and then he winced from the pain.

"I didn't do this. And what do you mean the back window?" She looked at her husband.

"I might have a cracked rib too. That was a baseball bat that hit the window first."

"Warner!"

Christian moved in closer to him. "You need to go to the hospital."

"Right. So they can put that on TV too?"

"Too?"

Warner let out a long breath and winced again. "This was all over Patty's show and the only reason the guy got upset is because her cameras were in the building today too."

Clara let out a gasp. "This is stupid, Warner. She's going to get you killed."

"I'm calling Curtis," Christian said as he pulled his phone out of his pocket. "You guys are sure putting a downer on my evening."

He took hold of Victoria's hand and held it up, showing them the ring on her finger.

"Christian!" Clara jumped up and passed right past her brother and to Victoria. "You're engaged! You're engaged!"

"Yes," Victoria said softly shifting her eyes to Warner and back to Clara. "It was very romantic."

The moment was short lived when Christian began to speak to Curtis. The room was quiet and they waited.

Christian ended the phone call and placed his phone in his pocket. "He'll be here in twenty."

"You didn't have to do that," Warner complained. "I'll be fine. It's not the first time I've had my face beat in."

"Well, I'll guarantee it'll be the last. We don't roll like this," Christian said through gritted teeth.

Clara smiled at her brother and then looked directly at Warner. "We need to call the police."

"They already took the guy in. He was stupid enough to do this as I left the building today. Security detained him."

"That's something at least." She crossed her arms in front of

267

her. "Don't you think this is reason for a lawyer? I mean if it's dangerous for you be on this show you should be able to get out of the contract."

Warner sat down at the table, shifted in his seat, and adjusted the towel on his cheek. "Actually, Jeremy said there was a call today about me. He wouldn't give me specifics, but he told me what they were looking for. He wants new material written."

"You mean someone wants to buy your songs?"

He shrugged. "It sounded bigger than that."

Clara moved toward him to pull him into her arms but stopped short when he tried to back away.

"I can't believe it. It's really going to work? This stupid show is going to get you signed!"

"Now, don't go saying that. This isn't how my life works out."

"It's time it does."

CHAPTER 44

*C*urtis arrived, just as promised, and Warner should have known he wouldn't travel alone. Before Warner knew it, the entire Keller family was in their living room.

"You're lucky he didn't break your cheek." Curtis placed a butterfly bandage over his eyebrow.

"He wasn't looking to kill me, just make me look bad."

"Well, you look bad." Curtis sat back and examined his work. "You're sure they took off with this guy?"

"Yeah."

Zach walked across the room, his phone in his hand. "I confirmed they arrested the guy. My lawyer thinks you should put a restraining order on him."

"I'll think about it."

Zach narrowed his eyes on him. "Think hard. And listen, you're covered with a lawyer if you need one to go after this guy."

"I appreciate that. I can't afford a lawyer and…"

"That's not what I said." He moved in closer until he was standing right behind Curtis. "We all work together here."

Warner contemplated that for a moment. "Okay. Thanks."

It was now past eleven and the front door opened again. This time it was Jeremy Smith.

Ed stood from his position on the couch with a menacing look to him.

Jeremy stopped walking. "I'm just wanting to check on Warner. Is he alright?"

"I'm fine," Warner called and the sea of Kellers between him and Jeremy parted.

"Holy crap!" Jeremy hurried to him. "You needed an ambulance. How did you even drive home?"

"Let's call it adrenaline."

Zach stepped up to Warner's side. "What's going to happen to the guy that did this?"

"He was arrested."

Zach nodded. "We know that. Warner isn't going to have to work with him further is he? If that's the case, it's not safe for him to be on your show."

Jeremy's eyes opened wide. "Oh, no. I wouldn't have the guy back. He's too much trouble. I can't have him beating everyone up who gets mentioned on another show."

"I'm serious," Zach continued and now Curtis and Carlos were standing right next to him. "If there is a chance that he comes back, and is near Warner again, my lawyers will be unleashed on your company. Warner is doing this show in good faith that it will lead him to sell his music. This isn't for the hype or to become some bad publicized reality TV personality."

Jeremy nodded sternly. "You have my word. Warner will be taken care of. He's my most promising talent. I have no reason to want him put in harm's way."

Perhaps it was the late night, the pain throbbing in his head, or sheer delirium from the situation, but Warner wanted to grin and laugh. Jeremy Smith had just said he was his most promising talent. That might have been one of the nicest things anyone had ever said about him.

.   .   .

ONCE THE HOUSE EMPTIED OF KELLER FAMILY, CLARA HELPED Warner up the stairs and to bed. She turned off the lights and crawled in next to him.

"Are you okay? Did that stuff Curtis give you help take the pain away?"

Warner smiled as much as he possibly could. "It's not the medication that makes me feel better. It's you. It was your whole family showing up here to take care of me. Me."

"You're one of us now."

He nodded. "And tonight I felt like it."

Clara took hold of his hand. "I'm afraid to hold you too tight.

"I'm just bruised."

"And bruises hurt."

"Yes—they—do." He finally laughed and then closed his eyes. "But did you hear what Jeremy said about me? I'm his most promising talent."

Clara laughed. "Out of everything tonight you're smiling about that?"

"Yes, I am."

"You deserve good things, Warner."

He wasn't looking at her, but her voice carried her truth and he knew in that moment she meant it. Maybe she could move on with him and not worry that his past would creep back in and destroy him.

THE NEWS STATIONS HAD QUICKLY PICKED UP ON THE STORY THAT Patricia Little's stepson had been beaten by one of the co-stars of his own reality TV show.

Clara turned it off the moment they began to talk about Patricia and her TV legacy.

273

"You didn't want to hear about me on TV?" Warner mused as he sipped his coffee at the kitchen table.

"Are you kidding me? I live in my own naive reality. And my story says you should see the other guy."

Warner winced when she said it. "You don't really think looking like this that I got one blow into him do you?"

She shook her head and rolled her eyes. "I said that was my reality. Don't mess with me."

He laughed, but there was a serious undertone to her voice.

"You leave on Thursday, huh?" He asked as he stirred sugar into this coffee.

"Yeah. I don't know if I'm ready for this."

"You're ready."

"We're talking thousands of people, Warner."

"And you've performed for thousands of people."

She let out a choked laugh and sat down at the table. "Not all at the same time."

Warner reached across the table and took her hand. "The lights are so bright it'll only look like you have a theater full."

"Comforting."

"I try."

CHAPTER 45

*C*lara packed her suitcase and repacked it. All of her outfits that she'd wear while performing were already on a bus and headed to the first leg of the tour.

"Did you sneak in some cheesy picture frame of your husband to put on your night stand?"

She turned to see Warner leaning against the doorjamb. He looked better already, though the black eye was going through that yellow stage, but the cut was healing nicely.

"My cell phone is full of them if that makes you happy."

"I'd really like to be at that first show."

"Can't you arrange that with Jeremy?"

Warner shook his head. "I've been out all week. He was gracious to do that."

She had to agree. Jeremy Smith had really come to Warner's aid since he'd been attacked. Not only had he given him time off to heal, he'd fielded most of the media. And he'd put everything in a good light—Warner didn't seem like a victim when Jeremy was done fielding reporter's questions. He had agreed with Zach though, and a restraining order was issued against the guy who had beat Warner up. She assumed Warner had agreed to it to calm her down.

Warner walked into the room and wrapped his arms around her waist and rested his chin on her shoulder as she continued to recount the clothes in her suitcase. "Ten cities—three and a half weeks."

"Seems like a lifetime."

"We do tend to rush things a little, so yea, it does seem like a lifetime."

Clara turned in his embrace and wrapped her arms around his neck. "This is it, isn't it? No matter why they put me on this tour, this is the time for me to show what we can do. These are your songs."

"They sure are and I can't think of anyone making them sound as sweet."

"I can. You'd make them that way."

He pressed his lips to hers gently. "Well then, here's my proposition. When you get back, we begin to record the songs as a duo."

"Mr. and Mrs. Wright?" she joked.

"Maybe."

Clara let out a sigh. "You should be going on this tour with me. We should be doing this as a team. I'm just waiting for the witch to come after me, but she hasn't yet. Because none of this makes sense, Warner. Who picks a person to perform at their concerts like this?"

"People do it all the time."

"I just didn't think it would ever happen to me."

He reached his hand into her hair. "Maybe that's why it did. You're not pretentious or needy. You do this for the joy of it. That comes across loud and clear."

"I love you. I'm going to miss you."

He kissed her again. "Make me proud."

~

CLARA RELAXED HER HEAD AGAINST THE SEAT ON THE CHARTERED airplane. This was nice, she thought. No lines. No extra fees, she laughed.

Trent stood above the vacant seat next to Clara with a beer in his hand after takeoff. "Would you like some company?"

"Sure." She smiled up at him as he sat down next to her.

"How's your husband doing?"

"He's fine." She relaxed again. "I assume you heard the news."

"Who hasn't? That was a low blow."

Sure was. "Some people can't take it."

"My wife is afraid something like that is going to happen to me."

Clara turned her head toward Trent. "That was selective. Is she still worried about you on this tour?"

"Yeah. See, she couldn't come with me because she's pregnant."

Clara lifted her head from the seat. "Congratulations."

"Thanks. I wouldn't get to be here if we weren't only doing a few shows."

She was glad it was only a few too. It would be enough to get some exposure and experience. But already she wanted to be back with Warner.

TRENT HAD BEEN GOOD CONVERSATION ON THE FLIGHT. THEY WERE a lot alike. They both had big families, were recently married, and wanted a house full of kids.

Trent had a lot more experience performing the kind of venue that they were headed to. He'd given Clara a few tips to ease her mind, but most of all, he'd given her a friend to turn to if she needed him.

Their first show was in Anaheim, California. Clara had

expected the weather to be much warmer, she was pleasantly surprised to find out it was rather cool in the fall.

They were expected to settle into their hotel rooms and then meet up for the bus to take them to the Honda Center where they would perform the first show of Savannah's tour tomorrow night. There would be a full run through and rumor had it that if they thought Savannah was critical of them during rehearsal, she was worse on the road.

The stress of being on the road with Savannah and her crew were lessened when Clara stepped into her room and there was a bouquet of roses and the card simply said, *I love you! Warner.*

She was missing him like crazy and it had only been a few hours. But since the night he'd been beaten up there was a new feeling that had emerged from this crazy, whirlwind romance she was having. The feeling was love, but on a grander scale and respect like she'd never had for any other person.

Ten cities and they'd be back together. His show would be wrapping up their taping and then they could be together. And for the first time since he chased her down in the street, they could find out about each other and she could finally date her husband.

The thought made her laugh.

Thanks to modern technology, Trent had given her a grand idea. She was going to Face Time with Warner tomorrow night so he could see and hear her perform live. It was almost as though he'd be there. She couldn't think of a better plan—unless she flew him out.

WARNER SAT ON THE COUCH LETTING THE FEELING OF HOME SINK in all around him. Only a month ago he had lived in the worst apartment ever and now he had a home and a wife.

His wife. God, wasn't she amazing? He'd just watched her

perform live at a concert in California thanks to the guitarist from The Broke Tourists. She killed it. His music had never sounded sweeter than when his wife sang it with her guitar.

He let out a deep breath when the phone rang.

"What did you think? How did I do?" Clara was screaming into the other end of the phone.

"Oh, sweetheart, I cried. I actually cried."

"I did good. I did really good!"

He could hear the excitement in her voice and it buzzed though him too.

"Jeremy said they had someone filming so they could put it on my show. You know, loser Warner's wife performing his music on tour with Savannah."

"First of all you're no loser."

"That's because I have a smoking hot wife."

"Well you do." She laughed. "Oh, Warner the energy that buzzes through this place is amazing. I mean sure, half the seats were empty when I took the stage, but still."

"They won't always be empty."

"Tom Wheeler says we need to get these recorded and soon."

"I happen to agree with him."

"Ten cities," she reminded him.

"Nine to go."

"I'll be home to you soon. I miss you."

"Not possibly as much as I miss you."

They finished their conversation and Warner ended the call. If there was as much energy buzzing through him, as she'd said, he wondered just how high on life she was at the moment.

He stood and headed for the stairs. He needed to get some rest. Randy had offered to meet him in the studio the next morning and help write some new material. Jeremy was still being tight lipped about who wanted to work with him, but he didn't care. Someone was taking note and he was going to impress them.

As he turned off the light and cleared the first few steps his phone chimed a new message in his pocket. He smiled. She was going to be up all night. He might never get any sleep.

But when he looked down at the message his heart rate kicked into an uncomfortable pace and his hands began to shake.

Today would have been her 33rd birthday. You killed my baby. I will make you pay.

It came every year in a letter, in an email, now in a text message. Patricia Little still blamed him for her daughter's death and he didn't have anything to do with it. But what did it matter? His life was in her hands as long as she possessed the power she had.

Warner slowly climbed the stairs to his room. His adrenaline and excitement from the night was ruined. Mindy had made her own choices in life and she chose to stay in Vegas when he came home. Her death was not his fault.

He fell onto the bed and closed his eyes.

It was never going to end.

CHAPTER 46

*C*lara stood on the side of the stage and listened to the band play after her. The lead female vocalists were amazing. They just had great sound together.

Trent looked toward her as they finished their song and smiled. He knew that feeling too, she could tell. There was electricity that just exploded inside of you when the crowd applauded.

Four more songs, then the four of them ran off stage as the crew began to tear down their set and set up Savannah's.

Clara was there to hug each of them as they came off the stage. "You were fantastic. Absolutely amazing!"

Starla, the dark haired singer said, "You were great too. A hard act to follow."

"I don't know about that, but thank you."

"I'm starving," Cheryl, the blonde who was married to the drummer, said. "They have food back here, right?"

"I love a woman who can eat," her husband said as they walked away with Starla.

Trent wiped a bead of sweat from his brow with his sleeve. "What did your husband think of your set?"

"He was thrilled. Thank you for thinking about doing that."

"Hey, what are friends for?" He fanned himself with his hand. "So you going back to eat too?"

"I want to watch her take the stage. I want to see that magic from here."

"Okay, I'll make Starla save you some food." He bent over and kissed her cheek then went on his way.

Clara certainly hadn't thought she'd made friends on this tour. She'd already had her emotional walls up and ready for attack. But what she was finding was that no one thought little of Warner, it was Patricia they hated.

WARNER AND RANDY WORKED FOR TWELVE HOURS IN THE STUDIO which Jeremy Smith had arranged for them to use.

Warner had to admit that doing the show had some perks. Of course Randy had to sign a million waivers to work with Warner and to acknowledge that he'd be videotaped for the show. That, Warner thought, was a pain in the ass.

As they wrapped up their day and put their instruments in the cases, Warner looked up at Randy.

"Thanks, man, for helping me out."

Randy closed his guitar case and looked at him. "I was really pissed at you. You're lucky I chose to do this."

Warner shook his head. "What?"

"I had it in my head you were moving in on Clara and using her. Then you run off and get married. That isn't like her."

"Well it seems to be her style now."

"Okay, let's just say it wasn't." He rested his hands on his case and leaned on it. "She fell for you the minute you sat in on her rehearsal and listened. I thought she was crazy." He looked at his watch and picked up his case. "I still think she's crazy, but she's in love with you so I give her credit. What I don't like is that she's on this tour, alone, and that bitch of a stepmother of yours has anything to do with it."

"She didn't know that either when she signed."

"I know. That's no one's fault. I just don't want that woman to hurt her. Who's to say she didn't order that attack on you personally?"

That thought had crossed Warner's mind too and he didn't like it.

"I think she'll be fine. Only eight more cities after tonight."

Randy laughed and headed toward the door. "You know, she owes me and now so do you. I think that first born kid needs my name. No matter if it's a girl or boy."

Warner laughed. "I'll let her know your opinion on the situation."

"I think she knows," he said as she walked out of the room.

As Randy walked out Jeremy walked in. "You guys got a lot of work done today."

"He's pretty talented."

"I think he was here for moral support. I was watching. You can crank them out can't you? How do you write that many songs?"

Warner shrugged. "It's just how I work, I guess."

"Keep it up." Jeremy said as he pulled up a stool and sat down. "How is your wife doing?"

"She's good. I had the pleasure of watching her performance last night on the phone."

"Technology is something, huh?"

"Yep."

"She has a few days between shows coming up, doesn't she?"

"Yes. She'll be home for three days next week."

"Good. I'll see if I can't get meetings set up during that time for you. It would be nice if she were here with you."

Warner focused his eyes on Jeremy. "You're going to tell me who's looking into my music?"

He smiled. "It'll be time by then." He stood. "They want to do interviews with you tomorrow. Be in there by ten?"

"No problem. And thanks for the use of the studio."

"Only the best for you." He gave him a wave and walked out, but Warner stood and stared at the door that had closed behind him.

He squeezed his eyes shut and hoped that Jeremy Smith wasn't just setting him up. He'd never had anyone, other than Clara, compliment him as much as Jeremy Smith did. It was nice, but Warner was skeptical.

CHAPTER 47

*C*lara was counting down six more shows, but after tomorrow night she could go home for a few days and spend time with her husband.

It was already growing colder in Kansas City, but when the lights on the stage hit she warmed up just fine.

After her set, which she thought only got stronger each night, she would stand off to the side and watch The Broke Tourists' set. It too sounded better every night.

"They are quite talented aren't they? More so than you or your worthless husband."

Clara turned to the woman who had spoken to her. It took her a moment in the shadows of backstage to realize that it was Patricia Little who was standing only a few feet from her.

Patricia walked toward Clara and her felt her body begin to shake. "I don't know what Jeremy sees in him—that show isn't going to help him advance his stupid career. Besides, if he gets a lucky break, he'll fail."

"No he won't." Clara's voice shook and she didn't want that. For Warner's sake she wanted to be strong. "Warner is the most talented song writer I've ever heard. He's going to do just fine, even with your harsh words."

"Harsh words?" Patricia moved in closer to her. "Do you know what he's done to me? Do you know the pain he's caused me?"

Patricia moved in even closer. Clara tried to back away, but she found she was already next to the wall.

"If you have a good marriage, I assume you've already heard about my Mindy."

Clara swallowed hard. "I've heard about Mindy. He told me everything about her."

"Yes, well, if he hadn't been the piece of trash he was, she never would have gotten into all that stuff and followed him to Vegas."

"She was already into all of that before she and Warner were together. You can't blame him for her death."

"You believe what you want to believe, but he's feeding you lies. They are all lies." She was so close Clara could feel the woman's breath on her skin. "He ran out on her when she needed him most."

"He left to pick up the pieces of his life. He changed."

"And he left Mindy there in the hands of that man who killed her."

"She took the drugs. She drank the booze."

The piercing stare from Patricia was frightening. The look in her eyes was just like that of Michael Hamilton's before his hand knocked her to the ground that night he tried to burn down the theater and leave her locked inside.

"What about the baby? Huh? Oh he didn't tell you she was pregnant?"

Clara was sure the woman had just kicked her in the gut.

"See, he's been lying to you the whole time," Patricia continued. "He's responsible for her death. And if you stay with him he'll be responsible for your death—even if it's only your career that dies."

Clara felt the tears falling down her warm cheeks and the breath in her lungs was coming in short bursts.

The sound of the crowd beyond them erupted in applause. Patricia looked out onto the stage and then back at Clara. "He's never going to change. He's going to lie to you for the rest of his life. And if you think a man can walk away from that lifestyle forever you're wrong. Dead wrong."

Patricia turned and walked way into the dark hallway that lead to the corridor just as the band cleared the stage.

Clara stood at the wall where Patricia had left her. The tears streamed down her cheeks and her body shook with the sobs.

Trent noticed her right away and hurried to her.

"Clara, are you okay? Oh, God. What happened?"

Clara could only look up at him. She could hardly even make out who it was, her sobs were so loud in her ears and the mascara running down her face had nearly blinded her.

Trent laid his guitar down and pulled her into his arms. "C'mon, it's okay."

She rested her head on his shoulder and wrapped her arms around him as he stroked her hair.

"Shh, get a breath in you."

Clara forced herself to breathe through her tears.

"What got you so upset?"

"Patricia Little," she managed to get the name out.

"Figures."

He held her tight and let her cry out her pain. When she felt as though she could breathe again Trent pulled back just far enough to look at her. She figured she was a horrific site, but he only smiled.

"Are you going to be okay?"

"I'm tired. I'm just so tired."

He smiled. "Let me put my guitar away and I'll see you back to the hotel."

He gave her a kiss on the top of her head and then walked away with his guitar.

Clara gritted her teeth. She wanted to believe Warner. She did believe Warner—or so she thought.

CLARA WAITED FOR TRENT AND HE HELPED HER TO A CAR THAT waited for them. The tears were back, but she'd managed to clean up the trails of makeup which had stained her face.

Trent let her rest her head on his shoulder and held her close as she cried out the rest of her tears.

When Warner called during their ride to the hotel, she silenced the call. She wasn't ready to face him. Not yet.

When the car pulled up in front of the hotel, Trent stepped out and held his hand out to help her from the car.

He walked her all the way to her room with his arm around her shoulders.

As she slid the key into the lock she turned back to him. "Thank you so much for being there for me tonight."

"Remember, that's what friends are for." He smiled kindly. "Are you going to be okay?"

"Yes." She let out a breath. "One more day and I can talk to him face to face. She just caught me off guard tonight."

Trent nodded. "I told you, she's a witch."

Clara laughed. "I don't think that was the word you used."

He nodded. "I'm trying to clean it up before that baby gets here and his first word is a four letter one."

"Your wife is very lucky to have you."

"I tell her that all the time." He kissed her on the cheek as he had the night before. "Goodnight, Clara. Call me if you need anything."

She nodded and closed the door.

Clara sucked in a long deep breath and slid down the door to the ground.

The tears were back, but this time they were angry tears and not aimed at Warner, but at herself for falling apart. If there had been a baby, Warner would have told her. If there was a baby, then he didn't know anything about that. Patricia Little had been trying to make his life hell since he was ten. Why wouldn't she go after the wife and make her second guess him too?

It was then her phone buzzed a text message in her hand. She looked down to see the words *I love you*. That was what she needed. Even if Warner knew about a baby, that was almost fifteen years ago. He hadn't killed her or a baby. Mindy had been a lost cause long before that. Warner fixed his life and Clara was proud to be his wife.

She texted him back. *I love you too.*

CHAPTER 48

$\mathcal{W}$arner walked into the interview room and sat down where instructed. There was a pitcher of water and a glass next to him so he poured some water and took a sip.

The interviewer began his questions and they discussed his writing and the songs he and Randy had penned the day before. They talked about Clara's performances opening up for Savannah.

He was so proud of her. And to think, he'd be holding her in his arms by tomorrow night. That made him smile and the interviewer even asked why.

"I miss my wife. But she'll be home tomorrow for a few days."

Within an hour they were done and Warner walked down the hall toward Jeremy Smith's office.

"Hey, you sounded good in there."

"Thanks," Warner said as he sat down in front of Jeremy's desk.

"So your wife comes home tomorrow?"

"Yeah. Can't wait."

"Ah, newlyweds." Jeremy laughed. "I set up a meeting for the next day, so don't be staying up all night, if you know what I mean."

Warner's phone buzzed a message and he pulled it from his pocket. "I will try to get some sleep," he said as he cleared the screen to see the message.

It was a photo, sent from the same phone number as the message about Mindy.

When the images came up, they were of Clara.

Warner felt his jaw tighten and the heat of his body rose.

There was his wife in the arms of that guitar player from the other band. Her head was on his shoulder. In the next picture he was kissing her head. But the one that had his blood boiling was them hugging in the doorway of her hotel room.

Another text came through. *Think she misses you? It's hard to remain loyal when you're on the road.*

Jeremy leaned forward. "Everything okay, Warner?"

"Fine. Everything is fine." But he knew that his voice conveyed his very thoughts. "Are we done for today? I need to get home."

"Yeah, yeah. Go. Let me know if you need anything."

Warner nodded, stood, and left the building. It would appear he had some packing to do.

HE WAS GRATEFUL THAT THE HOUSE WAS EMPTY WHEN HE GOT there. There wasn't much that was his and he wasn't a thief, so nothing would go with him if he didn't bring it.

The old mattress and bed they had stored in the garage was the hardest part to move by himself, but somehow he managed to get it in the truck.

As he filled up a box with his clothes, he heard the front door open. He winced. It would have been best if it was Clara walking in, but he knew better. He'd have to deal with Christian before he could even tell Clara that he didn't appreciate her blatant infidelity.

"Warner, are you up there?" Christian called up the stairs.

He winced. "Yes."

Nothing more was said until Warner hurried down the steps with a box.

"Did you give that old bed away?"

"No." He walked out the front door and carried the box to the truck. When he came back in Christian was waiting for him.

"What exactly are you doing?"

"Packing."

"Whoa!" He held his hand out to stop Warner from going up the stairs. "What's this about?"

"It's just best. I think we've made a mistake here and I'm just fixing it."

He tried to move past Christian, but he was quick. In a split second Christian had a hold of the front of Warner's shirt.

"Clara is kicking you out?"

"No. I'm leaving on my own."

"She didn't tell me this. If she'd have kicked you out we'd all be here helping you pack. What the hell is going on?"

Warner bit down on the inside of his cheek. He didn't like to call people out, but this called for desperate measures.

He pulled his phone from his pocket and showed Christian the pictures that had been sent.

Christian took a step back. "There has to be some mistake. Clara wouldn't…"

"Clara obviously did." He started back up the stairs and Christian followed.

"Man, this isn't right. We were not raised like this."

"Ya know, I'm tired of hearing how amazing the Keller family is. It looks like at least one of you made a mistake. Is that such a shocker?"

"Don't do that. You haven't talked to her have you?"

"No. When I called last night she didn't answer and now I know why."

Christian ran his hand over the top of his head. "Dude, this isn't how she rolls."

"It's not how I roll either." Warner gathered his toiletries and threw them into a box. "In fact, I shared with her everything I had ever done. I laid my whole life on the line for judgment and this is what I get in return. I don't know why I thought this would be any different."

He pushed past Christian and down the stairs. This time Christian didn't follow. He guessed he knew even his infallible sister might make a mistake too.

CHAPTER 49

*C*lara couldn't get on stage fast enough. She hadn't talked to Warner all day and she just wanted this show over so she could get home and see her husband.

She'd slept on Patricia's words all night and they just didn't add up. Somewhere deep down Clara knew she was lying about the baby.

If Warner knew anything about it, or even if it wasn't his, he was the kind of man who would have taken care of her. He wouldn't have let her stay and die.

"Clara! Clara!" Trent was running toward her.

"What? I'm going out."

"Don't you leave this arena until we are done. Do you understand?"

"Yeah," she said softly as she reached for her guitar. "Are you okay?"

"No I'm not okay. I'm so pissed right now I can't see straight. And you're going to get this fixed or so help me…"

They announced her. She had to go. But what was he talking about?

Clara nearly stumbled out onto the stage, looking back to see

Trent there with his hands fisted on his hips and his eyes narrowed on her.

She put on her smile and looked out into the arena. The filled seats were fewer than the shows before. Was word spreading that the girl and her guitar just weren't worth getting to the arena early enough for?

She'd done a radio interview earlier that day and warded off three different Patricia Little questions when they were asked. How did Warner manage to do that day to day?

Clara began her set and the few people in front of the stage were even singing along. Okay, the guy from the radio did say someone had posted her on YouTube.

The seating picked up as she cruised through her set, but Trent still stood on the side glaring at her. What could she have possibly done?

When her set was done she waved to the crowed, which had nearly doubled in size. There was no set to tear down for her so The Broke Tourists stood waiting for their turn. Each of them narrowed their stare on her.

"I know you want to rush home to your husband, but if you're not standing right here when I get off stage, I'll hunt you down."

The band was announced and they headed out to a thunderous applause. Their second single was racing up the charts and the crowd wanted to see them. But what was the mystery?

Tom Wheeler headed her way as she placed her guitar in its case.

"Sounded good."

Clara forced a smile. "Thank you."

"Listen, you've got a PR nightmare brewing. It needs to get handled quickly. You need representation and you need it quick."

"What does that mean exactly?"

"Consider working with me. I'd like to manage you, but then I could get a grip on this for you."

"I'm sorry. I don't know what you're talking about."

Tom pulled his cell phone out of his pocket and handed it to her. "These were released to TMZ today. Wife of new reality TV show star, who happens to be the stepson of Patricia Little, seen in a compromising position with another married band mate."

"Oh God!" She scrolled through the pictures on the website. "That's not what happened at all. I didn't do anything wrong. He was just…"

"No one wants to know just… They want to assume you ran off and married Patricia Little's stepson, toured with her lead artist, and then cheated on your husband. That's what they want to think."

"But I didn't. I didn't know her name would be associated with the tour and I didn't cheat on anyone."

Tom ran his tongue over his teeth and set a hand on her shoulder as he took the phone from her. "There's a car waiting for you outside. Get on a plane and get home. Be back to work on Wednesday with an answer for me on my representation for you. We need to get this nipped quick."

"This is why Trent is pissed at me?"

"He thinks you set him up. His wife is pregnant you know."

"I know. Oh, I didn't do this."

He nodded. "We'll get it handled."

CLARA KNEW SHE SHOULD HAVE WAITED FOR TRENT. SHE OWED HIM that kind of consideration. But she was flying back to Nashville and if she could get out and push the plane any faster she would.

She had, however, sent him a message apologizing for any damage done. She didn't know about the pictures and they were innocent. Nothing had happened. Of course he knew that, but now his name was tarnished.

There was another car waiting for her at the airport to take her home.

When she arrived, Christian and Ed were both sitting in the living room waiting for her.

"Nice to see you're home," Ed said, but his voice had an angry quiver to it.

"I'm home. Now where is Warner?"

"Moved out," Christian said from the couch, his back to her.

"Moved out?" She came around the couch and looked down at her brother. "He moved out and you didn't stop him?"

Christian stood and looked her in the eye. "You think I'd let him just walk out on you? He has valid reason. What the hell were you doing on that tour with that man?"

Now Ed was out of his chair too and they were both towering over her and looking down on her.

"I didn't do anything." She skirted around them and headed to the kitchen. She'd contemplated a glass of water, then a beer, oh hell—was there whisky? Deciding against everything she turned to her brothers. "I saw the pictures. I didn't sleep with the guy. I didn't kiss him. I didn't do anything. You have to believe me."

"No one has to believe you, Clara," Ed crossed his arms in front of him. "No one does believe you."

"Including Warner," her voice dropped.

She fell into a chair at the table and rested her face in her hands.

Christian sat down across from her. "What did you do?"

She looked up at him with tears now blurring her vision. "I didn't do anything. Patricia Little came after me telling me all this stuff about Warner and I broke down. He was comforting me."

Ed pulled out another chair, turned it backward, and sat down with his arms rested on the high back. "Someone set you up. Why tell you that and then stick around? I mean someone had to know you were going to seek comfort. They might have even known he'd give it to you."

"That's all it was. He was hugging me while I was sobbing, but funny you can't see that in those damn pictures."

There was a knock on the door and then it opened. Zach walked in with a stack of papers in his hand.

"Okay. I have my lawyers on this already."

The tears came harder now. "What are they going to do?"

"They're going to try and get those pictures taken down and we're going to find out who posted them. Next they are making amends with Trent and his wife. They too will want to fight this."

"Uncle Zach, I didn't do anything wrong."

He nodded. "I know. You'd never do that to the man you love. Who, by the way, is sleeping on the couch in my office." He threw her a set of keys. "Red one is parking garage. Round one is the elevator to my office. Don't lose them and be careful down there alone."

Clara jumped up from her seat and kissed Zach on the cheek. "Thank you."

CHAPTER 50

*W*arner was in awe of Zach's office. He'd never even lived in a place as nice as Zach's office. The Murphy bed had been pulled down. The flat screen TV rose out of the cabinet. Before he'd headed out, Zach had Chinese food ordered up and had his assistant fill the mini-fridge with water bottles.

Through the other door there was a full bathroom where Warner could even shower.

Warner shook his head. Everyone's life was so different.

He sat down on the couch and began to surf through the channels with the remote. Somewhere between an old episode of Full House and Guy Fieri he realized what the night in the office meant.

He couldn't just walk out on Clara no matter what she had done. He was part of a family now and families worked things out together.

Hadn't Christian tried to stop him? He'd made the call to Arianna who had called Randy who then had found him at the studio. Then it was Regan who met him there and drove him to Zach's office where Zach set him up.

Warner rubbed his stubbled chin. That was what a family did for each other—and they'd done it for him.

No one asked why. No one needed details. They had just stepped up.

Did they think he was a victim to Clara's infidelity? But did he really think that himself?

Warner turned when he heard the noise behind him coming from the elevator which Zach had left through. He must have come back for something.

Warner stood to greet his guest. When the door opened and Clara stepped out, his breath caught in his chest.

His first instinct was to run to her, scoop her up in his arms, and kiss her senseless. But he stopped just steps from her, tucked his hands into his pockets, and just looked at her.

She was still dressed in the outfit she'd performed in. Her stage make up had all been cried off, obviously.

"Hello, Warner."

"Clara."

She bit down on her trembling lip. "I missed you."

This was judgment time. He was going to sound like an ass, but he was still hurting so he figured it was justified. "Missed me enough to forget about me for a few hours."

She took a step forward and then stopped. "I didn't do anything. Warner, you gotta believe I didn't do anything to jeopardize our marriage or Trent's."

"Then what was that all about?"

Clara took one final step toward him until they were toe to toe. She looked up at him with weary eyes. "Warner, was Mindy pregnant when she died?"

Warner felt his body deflate as if he wasn't already empty enough.

She reached out and touched his chest. "Was she?"

"Patty got to you. She actually got to you."

"She cornered me at the concert the other night. She said you killed her Mindy by getting her into drugs and dragging her out to Vegas."

"She was already into drugs and I didn't ask her to go to Vegas."

"I know that. You know that. Patricia has a different story in her head." Clara sighed. "But was there a baby?"

Warner turned from her and ran his fingers through his hair. "There was a baby. That's what kept her in Vegas." He turned back to his crying wife. "But the baby wasn't mine. I may have been young and not smart about too many things, but I was smart about that. No matter what she'd ever tell me, I made sure I was covered if I was sleeping with her. Not so much to keep her from getting pregnant, but I didn't want anything she might have." He winced. "You know what I mean?"

Clara nodded.

"Anyway, she got knocked up, kept coming back to me when he'd kick her out. She wasn't too far along when she died. A couple months. I couldn't convince her to clean up. I couldn't convince her to leave with me either."

"Why didn't you just drag her away?"

Warner laughed. "You are a good person aren't you? She's been dead almost fifteen years and you worry about her." He walked back toward Clara and rested his hands on her shoulders. "She said my arguments were invalid anyway. She told me she'd miscarried and I had no reason to not believe her. After all, she'd never stopped using or drinking."

"You thought the baby was gone."

"I didn't find out she was still pregnant until after they did an autopsy and Patty came after me the first time."

Clara wiped her eyes. "Why didn't she ever use that for fuel before?"

"Because she knows it wasn't mine. She knows the truths. She just chooses to believe it's all my fault. I can't stop that."

"Why didn't you tell me about the baby?"

"It didn't seem relevant at the time. It wasn't my baby."

Clara wrapped her arms around his waist and he breathed in the scent of her as he held her tight.

"Warner, I didn't sleep with Trent. He was just comforting me because he saw how upset I was. He got us a car and he walked me to my room. That's all."

"I know." And he did.

"Come home. Zach already has lawyers all over this. Tom Wheeler wants to rep me and get his PR team on fixing this."

He pushed her back at arm's length. "You didn't sign with him did you?"

"No."

"Good. I don't trust him."

"Why?"

Warner shook his head. "He works with Patty. Why would I? Besides, day after tomorrow Jeremy has a meeting scheduled with whoever wants my music. He wants you to be there too. We were waiting for you." He pulled her in close. "But you're home early." He brushed a curl from her eyes. "And I think we are entitled to an entire day of makeup sex."

Clara smiled back at him then rose up on her toes. "Oh, I think we can certainly make use of that." She kissed him feverishly as though she'd missed him for years. Once again they'd escaped from Patty's evil talons, but when would it all hit the fan? One of them had to go down. Patty or them. With Clara by his side he was betting on Patty.

CHAPTER 51

$\mathcal{W}$ith Clara's hand in his, Warner walked into Jeremy's office.

"Welcome home, Clara," Jeremy said when they walked through the door.

"Thank you."

"I've seen the videos popping up of your performance. I'm impressed."

She smiled at the compliment. "I had some very good material to work with."

Jeremy nodded. "You sure did. Okay, are you two ready?" He grabbed a notebook off his desk. "Let's go meet your fate."

Jeremy led the way down the hall to a conference room and opened the door. No one was at the table yet, only a camera man and a sound guy in the corner.

"You two take those chairs and I'm going to sit over here."

Warner watched as the light on the camera turned on and Jeremy opened his folder with notes and papers.

Then the scent of cigar filled Warner's nose. He was always keen on the scent as it reminded him of his father. It was a moment later he heard voices in the hall and the sound of people convening.

When the door opened, four men walked through, whom he didn't know, but when the last man walked through Warner literally felt his head spin and he thought he just might collapse.

Harley Oxbury walked through the door bigger than life, a lit cigar stuck between his teeth.

In his older years he had begun to look more like Boss Hog than Nashville royalty, but the room obviously was still his with the direct attention being given to him from those around him.

His large cowboy hat was white with a rhinestone band and he wore a white suit. Warner didn't know anything about fashion, but it struck him as funny because he did know—from Patricia of all people—that you didn't wear white after Labor Day. But the OX could do any damn thing he wanted to.

Warner had never met the man, yet it was his demise that had caused Warner so much pain for so many years. Was it possible that Harley Oxbury was here to just seal the coffin?

"So you're Warner Wright, eh?" the OX asked through teeth still gritted around his cigar as he sat down and the others followed.

"Yes, sir. And this is my wife Clara."

"How do you do, sir?" she added.

"Wife? That must be new."

"A few weeks now, sir."

The OX nodded his head and then sat back in his chair and folded his arms.

"Warner, Mr. Oxbury is very informed on your music. He has seen video of your performances, and Mrs. Wright's as well," the man to the left of the OX said. "Mr. Oxbury is interested in signing you to a recording contract."

Warner's eyes were open wide and his heart was beating a million miles a minute. Clara gave his hand a squeeze and when he looked at her, she was trembling, trying to keep the smile she had concealed.

"That is very gracious, sir. But I wasn't aware that you owned a recording company," he said directly to Harley Oxbury.

"Just happen to have gotten into one." He leaned forward on his large arms, the cigar still burning between his teeth. "Ever heard of Master Records?"

Warner and Clara exchanged glances. "Yes, sir, of course. But I was under the impression that Jordan Farr and…"

He didn't get her name out before the OX shot his hand up to stop him.

"Let's say her name is like Voldemort. You don't say it aloud."

Warner didn't know if he should laugh at the joke itself or the Harry Potter reference from the older man. Instead he simply sat there stunned.

"It just so happens that in this town money talks, bullshit walks. You know how that works."

"Mr. Oxbury is now the sole owner of Master Records," the man said.

"Congratulations, sir," Warner added.

Harley Oxbury sat back in his seat again and crossed his arms over his massive chest. His eyes were on Warner.

"What do y'all say you leave me and Mr. Wright alone for a few moments? I'd like to get to know him."

Jeremy was the first to stand, collecting his notebook and papers. Harley Oxbury's group did the same.

Clara looked at Warner and gave him a gentle smile. She leaned in and whispered in his ear, "I didn't see this coming."

As she pulled away she gave him a wink and exited with the other men.

When the room was empty and the door had been shut Harley Oxbury stood up and unplugged the camera from its outlet.

"I guess they thought they'd keep that rolling. Not going to happen." He sat down in the chair Jeremy had occupied. "Comfortable?"

Warner nodded.

"Good. So let's get this out in the open. She's a royal bitch."

Warner tucked his lips between his teeth and tried not to smile, but the OX did.

"Fell for her hook, line, and sinker. Worst mistake I ever made." He took the cigar from his mouth and held it between his fingers. "You know you made the worst mistake of your life when your mistress is the one who sells the intimate pictures of the two of you to the tabloids."

Warner had never heard that side of the story.

"Well, cost me everything. I don't blame my wife for leaving me. And hell, she did good moving on if I do say so myself, but that hurt."

He took one of the glasses of water on the table, took a sip, and then extinguished his cigar in it.

"Okay, let's make this clear. This ain't about her. She's been messing with you for years and I know, because I've been watching. You have some talent, kid."

"Thank you."

"You would have been signed five years ago had she let you be. But no one wants to touch you because of her. You see that don't you?"

"Oh, I knew that."

"Jeremy knew you had some talent, though I think he thought it was only in writing. But I think you and your wife can bust into those charts and quick. Love Song hands down is one of the best songs I've ever heard."

Warner thought he still might die there with the man, but at least he'd die happy.

"So, I don't think she'll be messing with you too much longer, especially since she's going to be broke."

"How is that?"

"Her fortune was me paying her off. For years I've been feeding her to just let me be. She'd done all the damage she could do to me, but she shifted that to you." He tapped his meaty fingers on the table. "That show of hers is going to replace her with my ex-wife, which I think is as funny as hell."

Warner did let out a laugh there.

"I now own that company she bought into, but, son, a piece of business advice. If you only buy into something at twenty percent, you're not doing any favors to yourself. Some S.O.B. moves in and buys you out." That time Harley laughed.

"Anyway, this is going to air on your show. The world is going to know that you're my new talent now."

"You have no idea how much this means to me."

"Sure I do. I once had a recording contract myself, remember."

Warner chuckled. "Right."

"Oh, and I'm signing your wife too."

Warner had a giddy flutter in his stomach.

"A few more things," the OX continued. "Those pictures were taken by Tom Wheeler. Your wife is on the up and up."

"I know she is."

"Well, since you're our talent, and so is she, we plan to sue him for the libel. And Trent is in on that. His wife was so stressed it caused her early labor."

"Is she okay?" Warner inched over the table.

"Yeah. They got her stopped. He got to be with her."

That was the last thing Warner needed over his head. He was already upset that the world thought his wife had done anything with the man.

"When the tour resumes, Clara needs to finish out her contract."

Warner nodded. That made sense.

"But now that Savannah is signed with our house, we get to step in and make a few adjustments to the tour."

Warner nodded again. He figured they'd pull Clara from it. No one needed that distraction anymore.

"You'll be performing with her, so clear your schedule. We're also extending her run as opener."

"Really?"

"Unless you don't want to work with your wife."

"Oh, no. I can't think of anything better."

The OX winked at him and took another cigar out of this shirt pocket. "I thought so."

"I guess we'll let them in now." He stood and rested his hand on Warner's shoulder. "She's not going to bother you anymore, son. You're in my hands and the only thing people are going to read about you is your name on the top of those charts."

Warner's chest was going to explode his heart was still racing so fast. "Thank you, sir."

The OX nodded and walked to the door to open it.

EPILOGUE

$\mathcal{B}$y the twentieth night of Savannah's concert, the seats were filled when Clara took the stage. Wardrobe had redesigned her outfit to be even more stunning. Still in a flowy white shirt, it now sparkled with rhinestones. Her short white skirt, showed off too much leg, her father had told her, but with the boots and the hat, it made one hell of a statement.

"Hello, Denver!" Clara shouted and the crowd at the Pepsi Center reciprocated with a loud roar. "Let's get this party started."

Clara hit the first chords of the first song and her voice rang through the speakers. As she started the second verse another guitar added to hers and from the side of the stage Warner walked out, dressed in a black fitted T-Shirt, black tight jeans, and a matching black set of boots. The large brimmed, black, cowboy hat, shadowed his dark eyes, but they still smoldered when he looked at Clara.

His guitar strap matched hers, lined in rhinestones. Hers said Mrs. and his said Mr.

When their voices paired, the crowd was on their feet.

And as Warner's songs filled the arena, it was by the voices of those gathered to hear them. Everyone knew his songs thanks to the OX getting them recorded and air played immediately.

Clara smiled as she took a step back so he was spotlighted.

Their set was wrapping up when the monstrous drum beat began behind them. When the curtain rose, The Broke Tourists were there and the song grew in intensity.

Their vocalists moved forward and in between Clara and Warner. They were all singing his song and the crowd was eating it up.

Trent took his solo next to Clara, and she smiled as his notes rang through the arena.

"Ladies and gentlemen, The Broke Tourists!" She introduced them.

"And we are the Wrights!" Warner said. "Thanks for having us!"

As the band played on, Warner and Clara left the stage.

The moment they hit the side of the stage, Warner gathered Clara up in his arms and swung her in the air.

"I love you."

"I love you too." She kissed him hard on the mouth.

"I knew you'd be my ticket. You and that voice."

"Yeah, and your way with words."

Warner lifted his hand to her cheek and gazed at her with those lusty eyes. "Every song I write is a love song for you."

"Let's go back to the hotel," she said, taking his hand and walking away from the stage. "Maybe I can give you something to write about, Mr. Wright."

We hope you enjoyed Bernadette Marie's
Love Songs.
Continue the family saga with an excerpt from book seven,
Home Run.

HOME RUN

CHAPTER ONE

$\mathcal{T}$here was a pure energy in the car as they drove away from the arena. Christian Keller had it all, just when he thought he'd lost it.

His career-ending injuries were just the start to finding out he could keep going and that's what he was doing.

He'd just watched his sister perform with her husband, on stage at the Bridgestone Arena right there in Nashville. Hometown kids making it big time.

As his best friend Dave pulled out of the parking lot the number one country song came on the radio, and wouldn't you know it, it was Clara and Warner Wright, his sister and her husband.

Christian's fiancée, Victoria, hugged his arm and slid across the back seat as close as she could to him. "That was the best concert ever. Your sister and Warner were phenomenal. The Broke Tourists are one of my favorite bands. And that Savannah and her hair!"

Ashley, Victoria's sister, turned in her seat and looked back at her. "I know, right? Do you think we could buy hair like that?"

They both laughed, but Christian just took in the ambiance.

His career as a baseball player was over. He'd come to grips with that. It had caused him a lot of emotional and physical pain over the past year, but now Christian had new things to look forward to.

The team he'd played for was talking about him coming into the organization as management. The woman of his dreams had accepted his marriage proposal and wore his ring. And tonight, he'd take her home to the home he had built—for them. It was a surprise, and he had something very special planned.

"You know," Victoria continued. "Ali would love a Savannah wig. We should think about marketing them."

"My kids and their tastes," Ashley added.

Laughter filled the car and then a scream pierced the air.

A blinding white light forced him to cover his eyes.

CHRISTIAN SAT UP IN BED. HIS HEART WAS RACING. HIS FACE AND hair were wet. And he was alone.

He threw his head back against his pillow.

Of course he was alone. He'd been alone for almost a year and the replay of that night wouldn't give him any peace.

Christian rolled to his side and he looked at his phone on the night stand. It was five-thirty in the morning. He let out a grunt and rolled out of bed.

It took a minute for his knee to stabilize under him before he walked across the room. His shoulder ached, as it had since the surgery after the accident.

He flipped on the light in the bathroom and looked at himself in the mirror. The jagged scar on his forehead was beginning to fade, but it would always remind him that on that night he'd lost everything. His career. His best friend. And even if her life wasn't taken—he'd lost his fiancée.

Well that was life now. Victoria had a lot to deal with too.

Christian turned on the faucet and splashed his face with cold water.

Victoria's life had changed drastically when that drunk driver crossed the median. She'd lost her sister in that moment. Her leg was shattered. And she was the next of kin to her niece and nephew, whom she was now raising.

A single woman trying to advance her career and plan a wedding was now guardian to a two year old and a four year old —and he was no help.

Christian turned off the sink, and then turned on the shower and let it warm.

He'd been so overwhelmed with losing his best friend, he'd nearly lost his mind.

It wasn't losing him, it was watching him die and not being able to get free from the accident to help him.

Just the thought of it made Christian's heart kick start again.

He slipped off his boxers and climbed into the shower. No matter how hot the water was, it would never wash away the pain that day still caused.

By six-thirty, he was dressed and sitting in his quiet kitchen having a cup of coffee. The dress shirt and tie made him uncomfortable, but it was the way he had to dress for work now. He supposed he owed it to his brother and uncle for stepping in and giving him a job, though he didn't care much about construction.

Christian's entire family had stepped in when he needed them. There was no way to repay them. His sister Clara and cousin Avery were at his house daily to make sure he ate. His mother stopped by and cleaned the house. His future sister-in-law Darcy made him freezer dinners and stocked them for him.

It had been like this for a year.

When would it all ease so he could get on with his life?

PLEASE REVIEW

We hope you enjoyed *Love Songs* by Bernadette Marie. If you did, we would ask that you please rate and review this title. Every review helps our authors.

Rate and Review: Love Songs

ABOUT THE AUTHOR

Bestselling Author Bernadette Marie is known for building families readers want to be part of. Her series The Keller Family has graced bestseller charts since its release in 2011. Since then she has authored and published over fifty books. The married mother of five sons promises romances with a Happily Ever After always…and says she can write it because she lives it.

Obsessed with the art of writing and the business of publishing, chronic entrepreneur Bernadette Marie established her own publishing house, 5 Prince Publishing, in 2011 to bring her own work to market as well as offer an opportunity for fresh voices in fiction to find a home as well.

When not immersed in the writing/publishing world, Bernadette Marie can be found spending time with her family, traveling (mostly to Disney parks), and running multiple businesses. An avid martial artist, Bernadette Marie is a second degree black belt in Tang Soo Do, and loves Tai Chi. She is a retired hockey mom, a lover of a good stout craft beer, and might have an unhealthy addiction to chocolate.

www.ingramcontent.com/pod-product-compliance
Lightning Source LLC
Chambersburg PA
CBHW022207010726
47493CB00002B/454